THE CHRONICLER'S LAMENT

KANWAL KAPOOR

First edition

ISBN: 978-93-344-4196-3

Contents

2nd Day of Sinter, Year 10277 3rd CE

Here begins Volume XC-3211

Prologue

A sense of duty — above all.

The legacy handed to me.

Foolish as it may be. In my humble opinion.

In the main cavern of Satraksh, my home, stands the statue of the first Grand Chronicler. Surrounded by death and decay, it looks down upon me — Laahek, the last Grand Chronicler. Slumped at its feet.

At fourteen years, the youngest Grand Chronicler ever. A title I always aspired to attain. But in the end could not earn. A title I gained by being the sole survivor of the massacre that wiped out my people, the Krihaani, in a single day.

By being the coward who hid. Holding my breath beneath the dead weight of their corpses, while rabid raiders revelled in their cruelty. After a long uncertain period, with the hope that those maniacs have left, I stumbled through the network of tunnels that joined the caves of Satraksh.

Stumbling, and fumbling to find everything I would need to continue the sacred duty of my people. As their last representative in this forsaken world.

Now, my pen scratching on paper, the only sounds in the impenetrable silence. I serve penance for my cowardice.

Thankfully it will not be too long before I join my kin.

While I record the events of our world as they unfold, I realise this massacre was just the beginning. I see the Threads weaving, forming a pattern of one inevitable outcome — destruction.

In months, perhaps weeks, the barrier of Sukarsha will fall and the embers of life under its protection will succumb. And with that will come the end of the oath that binds my people. The oath to record the true history of our world.

It is a burden I do not take lightly. For all we record must be the pure truth, unadulterated by a single lie or half-truth. Not even by omission. Not like those *historians* under the patronage of kings and emperors. Boot lickers who would say anything to make their current patron appear the most righteous person in the world. No. Not like them at all. Could you imagine one such as those to disparage themselves in their own writing? None but a Chronicler would. Highlight their own cowardice. In their own writings.

The only omission permitted in our records till now was our existence. We had remained hidden from the eyes of the world. No Volume of the Chronicle, before today, mentions our existence. Upholding our belief that we were mere observers. Not actors who could shape the world.

Yet, as I look around in the fading light of the torches, I see the bodies of my people, bloodied and broken. The stench of decay, strong in my nose. It all raises doubt to this belief. Someone out there not only knew of our existence, but also considered us, as a race, to be dangerous enough to eradicate completely.

If only I could be pragmatic. I would abandon this place and spend the final days of our world doing something a young boy of my age should. Like jumping off a waterfall into the cool river below, or an adventure through a strange jungle. I have read hundreds of Chronicles about such places. Places abandoned for centuries, filled with treasures that could buy a kingdom. That could be something I would enjoy. Live like a king in the final days of the world.

If only.

But I am not. If nothing else, the one thing I learnt from my parents was to put my duty above all. As the last Krihaani, the duties of the Chronicler fall on my shoulders.

I resisted the temptation to say broad shoulders. That would be an obvious lie.

And lies have no place in these Chronicles.

These chronicles are all that I have left of my people. The only thing that keeps me sane in these silent ruins.

And so, we begin. Without the fanfare that always accompanied the beginning of a new volume, the last Chronicle of Prathak. The one where the world is dying, and I am but a passive observer...

Chapter 1

Before we observe the fall of Prathak, indulge me while I begin by referring to few lines from the past.

About an event that happened thousands of years ago.

FROM THE NOTES OF CHRONICLER PAURAK

In the fortified Towers of Sriki, once a supposedly minor stronghold of the dreaded Halmvar.

Now far beyond the reach of Sukarsha's barrier.

Atop Sriki's highest tower, a battle takes place. A small Vah'ron strike force, merely five in number, takes on a hundred Halmvar armoured and armed to the teeth. The Vah'ron seem to have the upper hand, but not for long. I do not know if it was courage or desperation that led them to this ridiculous endeavour. But there they were. Fighting their way towards an objective known to them alone.

And the hundred Halmvar fighting them. Probably.

One would expect that the Knot which gave rise to all the active Threads today would be important enough for Chronicler Paurak to observe diligently and not reduce it to a single footnote. Putting it down as a foolish and ultimately futile attempt by the Vah'ron to destroy a minor Halmvar stronghold.

Had he done his duty, Perhaps the Krihaani would still be alive. Perhaps my parents would still be by my side. And I would not be sitting alone writing a Chronicle in a cavern surrounded by the silence of my people's mortal remains.

But...

Hindsight is always crystal clear. At the time no one could have predicted that this one single battle would set off a chain of events. Hurtling our entire world along a catastrophic path that would culminate thousands of years later with our destruction.

Not when hundreds of battles raged on, without signs of cessation, across all the lands of Prathak.

Not from one insignificant battle fought thousands of years ago.

Prathak is very different today. Everything has changed.

The Halmvar are long gone.

The Vah'ron are long gone.

But the seeds of destruction they sowed in their time have fully blossomed. Beyond what either of them could have possibly envisioned.

Today we are confined under the impregnable barrier of Sukarsha, created by the strongest magicians of the Vah'ron. An act that cost them their entire civilisation. Without their timely intervention the Halmvar's final act of desperation — the release of uncontrolled chaotic magic that destroyed life across Prathak — would have taken us as well.

The fall of the barrier would be catastrophic.

As I am sure you know.

I assume.

I mean, you must realise that this is just a book. Thus, I am always going to work with the premise that whenever I ask you something, you are going to give the exact answer that I want you to give. Makes my life so much easier. This is not a choose-your-own-adventure sort of book you know.

So, with all that glorious information, I am certain you can guess what comes next—

Correct!

Sukarsha is failing. There are already signs of the barrier weakening at its edges. Uncontrolled magic leaking through to wreak havoc. Abnormal fauna, spontaneous explosions out of thin air and swaths of dead flora to name a few choice instances. The stuff of nightmares. For some.

Now that you know where we are headed, let's Connect to the Threads and view first-hand the tapestry of doom that they weave. One inconspicuous pattern at a time...

Chapter 2

Thread: Rakh

Location: Anthala Crater

As the sun rises, the silhouette of a man emerges along an outcrop over the Anthala crater — unmoved by the wind that howls across. Dressed in a brown jacket and dark trousers, he would have blended into the surrounding landscape, if not for the glint of morning light reflecting off the ornate red scabbard at his side. Despite the strong winds, he stands unmoving, fists clenched by his side. His eyes scan the crater in front of him, taking in every detail. His rugged face shows signs of pain and sadness as if the crater was a wound on his own body.

His trance is broken by a low hum coming from a ring on his right hand. Snapped out of his stupor, he looks at the ring and as a subtle frown forms on his forehead, he rolls his eyes. He hesitates a moment before lifting his hand and lightly touches the ring with his left index finger. Instantly a wispy figure materialises in front of him from thin air. It looks roughly humanoid, though its form flickers too much, as if a reflection on cloudy and disturbed water.

Sounds come out of the floating figure, but they can only be heard as clicks. An occasional screech thrown in for good measure.

Belying his visible annoyance at the disturbance, Rakh speaks up with a calm voice, "Hold on. I am right at Anthala's edge. Let me move away."

> That is right. The very first words spoken in the first Chronicle I write are "Hold on." I had hoped for something tragic, something dramatic. I would even settle for good old cliched heroic words. Like "I will save you!" But no. As my luck would have it, I get "Hold on".
>
> Very well. I will "hold on" to the edge of my seat. Can't wait for more exciting pearls of conversation!

True to his words, Rakh moves a hundred steps away from the outcrop. Even though the figure still flickers, its voice is clear. It's a feminine voice. Impatience clear in its tone.

"Rakh, do you have the artefact in your possession yet? The Eyes are having difficulty tracking it so close to Anthala."

"Not quite yet," comes the succinct reply.

Despite its unclear form, it is obvious that the figure is quite annoyed. Thin wispy appendages on either side, probably arms, rise in the air, and fall in exasperation.

With a raised voice, she asks again, "What *exactly* do you mean not quite yet?"

Maintaining his composure, Rakh says, "I mean, I almost had it wh..."

"Almost? Not quite? You are at the origin of Sukarsha. If the artefact activates there, we all burn. So, how about answering the question directly!"

> You tell him, lady. Is it a lady though? Could be a thing? Or...maybe something unimaginable? Probably just a lady though.

After a few tense moments of silence, with no response forthcoming from Rakh, she speaks up again, "Well? Answer me."

"I will; if you let me get a word in. One of these days I will finish speaking before..."

"This is no time to get snide with me! Are you waiting for the Nirdak to come give you company?"

"A bird took it!", Rakh says quickly before the figure can interrupt him again.

"A bird! You let a bird get the better of you!"

Immediately, the air fills with a sound of laughter. The figure is shaking uncontrollably in sync with the laughter.

"The mighty Rakh. Bested by a bird. Maybe I should replace the Talons with a flock of birds. Then I won't be so overwhelmed in trying to manage this difficult group of people. In particular, *you*!"

With a sigh, Rakh speaks up again, "It's not as if I *wanted* to come on this mission by myself. But the Eyes promised that the artefact was just *lying there* for the taking. So, you sent your fastest Talon. And aren't you forgetting that this is Anthala? The birds here are anything but ordinary. The one that took the artefact would snap you like a twig if you ever interrupted it."

"Hrmph, enough idling around. Retrieve the artefact at once and contact me as soon as you are out of Anthala's influence. There is a serious matter we must discuss."

"What kind of serious..."

The figure disappears before Rakh can finish his sentence.

"Goodbye then.", Rakh speaks to no one.

Rakh looks at the crater again. A split second later he turns around and sprints away towards the roots of a gigantic tree.

> And I mean gigantic. I do not, cannot, exaggerate. It is quite literally impossible to do so in the Chronicle.

At a dozen paces from it, the tree almost fills his entire vision. The large size of the tree is most likely due to its proximity to Anthala. The magical forces here have been known to have unpredictable effects on the surroundings, and this tree stands as proof.

The tree's bark is very smooth, almost to the point of being reflective enough to see one's face in it. Removing all possibility of footholds along the base or the lower part.

Even if one could, somehow, manage to make it halfway up the tree where large branches start sprouting out of the main trunk, the branches would be too far apart for anyone to be able to jump up from one to another.

On most days skies of Anthala would be covered with clouds. Hiding the top of the tree. Today fortunately for Rakh, it is clear. Near the top, a large bird is circling a branch — its form indiscernible at this distance. Most likely its nest and, the very place where it would have deposited its recently acquired prize — the artefact. The current source of Rakh's problems.

"One of these days, I will have the great honour of retrieving an artefact that will be conveniently placed on the mantel in a nice and comfortable inn," Rakh says to no one, but himself.

And me. But he doesn't know that yet.

"Well let's just get this done," Rakh says aloud and as the winds around him pick up, he proceeds to stand still as a rock.

Let's see, we have a mountain playing pretend as a tree. No way up. And a bird that has already bested Rakh once.

No wonder he meditates. Probably a prayer to the gods above for the ability to fly, right?

I am sure they will fail him as they failed my people.

Chapter 3

Thread: Ridsan

Location: Isle of Jvala

While Rakh prepares for, what I can assume will be his inevitable failure to outsmart the bird, I have a question for you.

When are you reading this book?

Does Sukarsha still stand? Am I still alive? Are you?

How did you find this book? And spare me the lies. It does not matter how well you think you might have hidden your truth. All the patterns in the tapestry of Prathak are laid bare to a Krihaani.

Oh! Look at that. I think Rakh just twitched a little. I think Rakh is going to try to fly his way to the artefact now.

But before his fall, a short detour.

The isle of Jvala. One of the two islands that are safely enclosed within the barrier of Sukarsha. Smaller of the two, it lies a stone's throw away from the coast of the larger island of Sukarsha. The one the barrier is named after. It is home to but a few hundred dwellers.

A dormant volcano in the middle of the island the only thing of import here.

Thousands of years of silence is broken by a slight tremor. No one seems to care.

A whimper unnoticed by all amongst the screams of the thunderstorm above.

By all but Ridsan. Camped near the base of the volcano, feeling the ground through his bare feet. His old bones, used to the silence of the land for decades, are jolted by the anomaly.

He starts sweating profusely. Hands trembling as the sounds of provisions being thrown together fill the air.

He flees his makeshift camp. Stumbling and falling, as he makes his way towards the sounds of the island port, yelling at the top of his lungs.

"She awakens! Flee!"

> But who will listen to someone who can neither see nor hear?
>
> He might as well be a Chronicler.
>
> Another Thread observed dutifully. I hope.

And now we head back to Rakh. As he attempts to best a bird that has already outsmarted him. Will he fall? I say — yes!

Chapter 4

Thread: Rakh

Location: Anthala

Rakh is right where we left him. Standing still as a rock in front of an insurmountable tree, trying to figure out a way to get to its top, and get the artefact from a terrifying giant bird.

It has been hours.

The sun is almost at its zenith, and the wind has died down.

Without warning he springs to life and takes off his jacket and shoes. He feels the earth through his feet.

> For a moment there, I thought… never mind. I am seeing things. Here, all alone in this deep cavern. Once a thriving polis of the Krihaani. And now just me. Outside the Threads, the darkness and silence weigh heavy on me. Suffocating. It… It does things to your mind.

After going through some stretching motions, he instantly breaks into a headlong sprint towards the tree. A split moment before he is about to crash into the tree, he adjusts his steps to start running up the trunk. He is almost horizontal as he runs up the smooth bark. When all of a sudden, Rakh disappears in a purple flash of light. In an instant he appears tens of feet up. Continuing his sprint as if on level ground. His momentum pushes him forward along the surface. Another few running steps, and another flash. He continues his ascent until he makes an easy landing on one of the lower branches. He pauses at the branch to catch his breath. The combination of using his Focus and sprinting continuously take their toll.

> Oh, before you start feeling smug over a fourteen-year-old being wrong about something, you should know that a Focus like this has not been recorded in a very long time. There are exhaustive archives lined with all the Focus that survived Sukarsha's rise. None of the Paurnik focus appear in it.
>
> We believed them to be complete. Yet here we are. Another glaring example of one of the Krihaani's several false assumptions. All that have decided to rear their ugly heads at once. At least one having led to dire consequences.
>
> As you already know.

From his position, Rakh can now make out the nest quite clearly. Four, maybe five more flash jumps and he will be that much closer to the artefact. That much closer to danger. He takes a quick survey of the skies around the tree to make sure that the bird isn't near. He crouches down and springs up into a high jump.

Just before the apex of his jump he flashes inches above one of the higher branches and lands on it with poise. Repeating the manoeuvre until he is at level with the nest.

Even near the top, the branches are quite large. Taking a moment for another breather, Rakh observes the tree closely. No leaves. No flowers. No fruit. Nothing but barren branches, jutting from the massive trunk all the way to the top.

Nothing to break his inevitable fall.

Rakh stands close to the trunk, and the nest and the artefact still lie a good hundred steps away along the branch. Not wanting to look down and weaken his resolve, Rakh focuses on the artefact, to the exclusion of all else. Carefully, step by step Rakh reaches the nest. He looks at the artefact. It is about the size of a closed fist. Intricate patterns cover its surface. Placed in lines emanating from a single point on the top to another on the bottom. A dull blue-green glow pulses across the patterns in a slow rhythm. Except for a small and dark circular spot on its bottom half — a dead spot marring its exquisite beauty.

Just as he picks it up, huge claws swipe at the artefact. Startled, he loses his grip, and his balance.

Both Rakh and the artefact fall off to plummet towards the ground below.

"This bird got me twice on the same day. I'm slipping in my old age."

> Falling towards his inevitable death and still finds time to make a pun. Maybe I will grow to like him.
>
> If he survives.

As the ground gets closer, Rakh looks around furtively. His eyes scanning the tree as barren branches whoosh past him. Trying to find something to break his fall. But he knows better. He has observed the tree for hours. There is nothing.

And more importantly, the artefact is falling right along with him, giving him company on his short trip down.

"Can't use the Focus so close to the artefact. No idea how it might react!"

Neither of them can survive the fall.

> Is Sukarsha's end closer than I thought?

Rakh repositions himself to face the ground head-on. Bringing his arms closer to his body to descend faster towards the ground. As his legs fly past the artefact, he gives it a strong kick upwards. Creating a large gap between him and the artefact. Mere two feet before he is about to smash into the ground, a purple flash envelops Rakh and disappears. Above, the artefact continues to plummet towards the ground. Barely moments before the artefact would've crashed into the ground, a flash appears right above the ground and Rakh appears out of thin air moving upwards at great speed. The flash disappears and an instant later Rakh reaches the artefact and grabs it out of the air. With the artefact in hand, he makes a hard landing on the ground below.

Without waiting to give the bird another chance to attack him, Rakh moves to pick up his discarded coat and weapons. He sprints away from the tree. The wince on his face and the slight limp in his gait hinting at his close call.

> I was half right after all. I knew he would fall from the tree. Let's call this one a draw!

An hour later, once Rakh is confident of being far enough from Anthala and the bird, he sits on the ground next to a large boulder. Breathing hard, he takes a moment to feel his legs and hands. Confident that nothing was broken he leans back to the boulder and calms himself down.

Taking the time he needs to catch his breath, he stands back up. Though a sharp-eyed Chronicler like me would note that his stance is a bit lopsided. His arms hand by his side instead of one on his sword, the same Chronicler would not find a hint of pain or fatigue visible on his face. He scans his clothes and nods to himself. Satisfied, he activates the ring on his hand. Away from the crater's influence, the figure that materialises is pristine and almost lifelike. Were it not for the slight translucency, one could easily assume that she was standing right here in front of Rakh.

Name: Unknown

Affiliation: Talons of the Firebird

Rank: Zirsa

> No, her name isn't Unknown. It's just hidden. Even from a Chronicler's Glean. It should have revealed everything Rakh knows about her. Not just her name. But her entire past. Everything is hidden from me. Everything she was before she became Zirsa.

"I assume you have the artefact in your possession now?"

Rakh starts to speak but, before he can make as much as a grunt of acknowledgement come out of his mouth, he is interrupted.

"Or should I assume that one of the cottontails have outwitted you now?"

"The cottontails are larger than most men, not to mention smarter. But no, I did not get outwitted by one. "

"This time" he mumbles under his breath.

> He thinks no one heard it. But I did. Not only that, but it's also now and forever recorded in a

Chronicler's writing that Rakh got outwitted by a cottontail. I shall have to Delve into this when things are quieter. Not the best use of a Delve, but hey, end of the world. No oversight. I can do. What. Ever. I. Want.

"Enough with the muttering! There is a crucial piece of information I must share." She pauses. Expecting an interruption or a quip from Rakh. Pleased with the absence of the likes, she continues, "The Eyes have Seen two unknown Focuses. In Svarka"

Rakh shrugs his shoulders and replies, "So? Just send Suthrin and Donas to get them. If I remember correctly their current mission is close to Svarka"

"Perhaps you did not hear me clearly, the Eyes have Seen two *un...known... Focus.*", Zirsa says with emphasis. "Not some random artefact," she continues, "It's been years since a new Focus was discovered, let alone two. Except for you and I, none of the Talons alive have encountered an unknown Focus before. They would not know how to acquire them without running the risk of terrible consequences."

Rakh starts to say something but is once again interrupted by Zirsa, "I am sure you remember your first acquisition. I am sure half of Dankar remembers it."

Interesting.

One more Delve for the list.

Her eyebrows are furrowed. She moves her hands to her temples as if nursing a headache. Eyes closed in deep thought.

Rakh in a moment of wisdom, chooses to stay silent.

"Hmm," she sighs, "Besides, Suthrin and Danos were already on the way back to the grove. It will take them at least four days to reach Svarka. We cannot afford to wait that long."

"Zirsa," Rakh starts, "It will take me *more* than that to reach Svarka. *Twice that*," he says in a cajoling tone. As if a parent trying to tell their child *no* to one of their pesky demands.

> I have heard that tone plenty. Very ineffective in my experience.

"Not if you use your Focus. You could be there by the break of dawn tomorrow."

> See? Ineffective.

"What? Have you lost your mind?" Rakh exclaims.

Zirsa winces at the outburst. She looks away from Rakh. Not wanting to meet his eyes. She was expecting this.

> I am with Rakh on this one. From Anthala to Svarka. He will barely be able to breathe with the effort it will take him to travel that distance in such a short time. The physical drain this can cause might even be life-threatening!

Rakh takes hold of himself. He raises his hands in frustration.

"OK. Out with it Zirsa. What is it that you are not telling me? Even you would not be so impatient as to make me take such a huge risk for acquiring two Focus. Not ones that were discovered, by my best estimates, mere hours ago? What is going on?"

"Both Focus were discovered yesterday evening," Zirsa says in a petulant manner.

"In the 20 hours since their discovery, they have been in almost constant motion."

Zirsa once again expected the sudden shock in Rakh's eyes. There is a subtle change in his stance. He is ready to jump into action. His right hand moves to rest on his sword's hilt. He is alert.

This is an unexpected detail.

She continues, "The Eyes have always been foremost in discovering the artefacts and Focus. But this time, someone, somehow, has discovered them simultaneously or maybe even before the Eyes."

"By any luck, it could just be some random person who does not know what he holds," Zirsa says. Her head unconsciously shaking in denial.

Rakh raises an eyebrow, teeth clenched. "Luck has seldom been on our side Zirsa. You and I know that better than anyone else," he says in a seemingly calm tone. Not willing to put into words his fear of what the reality is going to be.

Zirsa on the other hand has no such qualms. She nods and says, “All the unknown Focuses discovered so far have always been well guarded. Hidden from the common man’s eye. So more than likely, the one who has these Focuses is going to be a...”

“Nirdak.”

Rakh says as if the word itself was poison. His nostrils flare as his eyes stare of in the distance. On his side his hand clenches the hilt of his sword tight enough to lose colour.

> The spite in his voice when he utters that single word gives me shivers. Everyone hates the Nirdak. Even us Chroniclers had a difficult time being unbiased while recording their deeds. But there’s something more here. Not a simple hatred formed of their reputation alone.

Zirsa nods her head in agreement and spluttered on, “It is of utmost importance that you reach Svarka as soon as possible. Time is of the essence. Despite our best efforts, the Eyes are unable to See what the Focus can do. You must....”

She catches herself mid-sentence as she observes Rakh’s questioning look. This was not her. She was the leader of the Talons. She takes a deep breath. Regaining the façade of being calm, she continues, "Even for a Nirdak, it will take them days to figure out how the Focuses work. We must get them back before they can do so. There is no telling what could happen in the time they experiment."

Rakh is already deep in thought, but there is a flicker in his expression at Zirsa's words. He silently nods and turns to face the direction of Svarka.

Even from Anthala, one can see the edge of Sukarsha. Though it blankets the sky, it is barely discernible. But near the edges, there is something more. A continuous movement in the barrier, which makes it visible to the naked eye. Perhaps it's the constant bombarding of the magical storms that rage outside the barrier. Or perhaps it's the barrier simply drawing its energy from the ground below. At its base a short distance away from the absolute edge, he could see the smoke from chimneys. Svarka. The only settlement still foolish enough to stay this close to the edge.

Zirsa casts a glance at the artefact in Rakh's hand. She is about to say something but thinks better of it.

"Good luck," With these last words Zirsa's image flickers away.

Rakh secures the artefact in a pouch at his side. Zirsa's warning — and the unknown Focus — have given him cause for concern.

He vanishes in a flash of violet light and reappears mid-air. As he falls, he carefully adjusts his direction and flashes ahead. And again, and again.

The world around him is a blur. Far ahead Svarka awaits.

> Even simply following him through a Connection is nauseating. I think I will rest now. Looks like the end of the world is going to be very exciting and I will need my energy.

Chapter 5

While Rakh went on his urgent and life-threatening, but altogether monotonous journey, I decided to get rest. Connecting to Threads *and* scribing is quite exhausting. As the only Chronicler, I must record everything of import, all by myself.

Normally the Chroniclers would work in teams, one to Connect and dictate, two others to scribe without interruption.

For obvious reasons, it is no longer a possibility.

Not to mention the number of teams has drastically reduced too. From tens of teams working at a time, it's now just — one. One critical team of one.

Therefore, like I said, I got much-needed rest. The lone burning torch in the chamber went out while I slept. And now, I... I keep having a strange sensation at the edge of my senses. That, I — might not be alone in here.

There are no sounds that I can discern. Except for the ones I make. No signs of movement as I scrounge for provisions in the dark. Only an instinct. Creeping. Gnawing at my consciousness.

The Chronicle.

The Threads.

They are my only means of solace now.

As I Connect to the Threads, I feel a connection to my predecessors as well. Those whose writings filled countless volumes of the Chronicle. Futile as those efforts were.

As I open the Chronicle, the Threads appear around me.

Bright, prismatic, boundless. Connecting everything across distance and time. Even you and me.

They engulf me. Like a cocoon. Like a barrier.

Every breath, every action, every thought of anyone on Prathak spawns a thread. I see them. All around me. A vast majority of them fade away, merging into the darkness. Inconsequential. Affecting none but themselves. Layers upon layers of threads, devoid of spirit. Of passion. Countless threads forming and fading away in the blink of an eye.

But few, such as Rakh's, shine with the brightness of a sun. Affecting everything they touch. The flourish in the tapestry, without which Prathak would be a dull bland pattern of mediocrity. These are the Threads which shape the future of our world. The ones we observe through the Chronicle. In the now, in the then and more. As I Connect to these, the spirit within, the fire in them, fills me with hope. Fleeting, false hope. But hope all the same. Their successes, their failures, I share them too. Make them my own.

Speaking of successes, I did get through my Delve list. Almost completed it. Another one of these journeys for Rakh, and I might just finish it off.

And speaking of failures, would you believe that all it took was a pair of carrots and one mud ball for a cottontail to fool Rakh?

Or maybe you would? Here you are reading this book after all. I assume there is not much else for you to do after the world has ended but read this book?

Why though? How did you even find this book? It's not like I am going to make any attempt to safeguard these. The world could end at any moment. What's the use? No one found our writings useful. Even at our peak. No one was interested in these books not even the authors themselves. The only reason these books were created was to perform our duty.

I could pick a thousand volumes that have been untouched after the last words were written in them. Gathering dust in forgotten corners of the archives. Thousands of years of writing, all for nothing. In the end, it doesn't even matter.

I wonder.

If instead of sitting here and writing words none will find useful, I should venture out in the world. Find a way to carry the knowledge of the Krihaani with me. Become the first Krihaani, to be a Thread, in the history of Prathak. Become the first Krihaani oath breaker.

No.

No. I cannot.

There is nothing that could make me abandon my duty as a Krihaani. I will not go into the afterlife only to face the disappointment of my parents. Had enough of that while they were here.

Mark my words though. Before the end of the world, I *will* find out who you are. You think you can hide from me in the future. You are wrong.

As wrong as my good friend Rakh is about entering that inn in Svarka all alone.

Chapter 6

Thread: Rakh

Location: Svarka

The only inhabited place under all Sukarsha that lies this close to the barrier's edge. One can stand on any of Svarka's rooftops to see the barrier emerging from the ground and curving overhead. It's a sight few dare witness in such proximity. With all the strange events that continue to happen close to the edge of the barrier, most Sukarshan decided to move several miles inwards. But not the people of Svarka. They saw opportunity where others saw only danger. And thus, we get — Svarka. The illicit trade capital of the three lands. None of the three powers that control Sukarsha care for what happens here, as long as they get their determined tithe on time.

And it is in this seedy settlement. In a seedy neighbourhood, in a seedy lane, Rakh stands at the entrance of a seedy inn.

> Do not bother asking which one. Svarka is all seedy neighbourhoods.

He is looking around for watchers. Satisfied that he has located all the competent ones, and, that they are not competent enough to harm him, he opens the door to the inn.

As soon as he steps inside a man sitting in one of the dark corners of the inn looks up. He eyes Rakh and quickly moves towards an inner room.

Rakh stays put near the entrance.

> Obviously waiting for the welcoming waiting staff of this esteemed establishment to take him to his table.

The room itself is poorly lit with dim overhead lanterns. Except for one, all the tables are occupied by excitable patrons. Drinks flow freely across the room. Loud conversations, and louder fights fill the air. There is no dearth of activity. I suppose those who live on the edge of danger both figuratively and literally know how to live each moment to the fullest.

Moments later a large man steps out of the inner room. The room falls silent in an instant. The patrons avoid eye contact with him. Shuffling uneasily in their seats. Those near the door jump out of the way at the mere hint of him moving forward.

If a wall could move, it would look exactly like this man. He is tall. Tall enough that he had to lean to almost half his height to get through the door. He is wide and muscular, wearing dark green clothing. His shirt, if that's what it's called, is hanging loose on one side near the hips. The buttons go diagonally across his chest instead of the normal central straight line. He does not seem to be armed. Although, the fear with which the other patrons look at him suggests he does not need any.

He looks to the inn's entrance and as his sight locks on to Rakh, he stiffens a little. His face remains frozen like a mask. He signals the others to continue what they are doing and lumbers towards Rakh. There is no hint of haste in him. He might as well be taking a walk along a lake.

As he approaches Rakh, he casts a shadow on Rakh's face coming from the overhead lanterns.

> Rakh has a thing for standing in front of gigantic specimens of a variety of species it seems.

"Leave," the man says with a booming voice.

The other patrons flinch at the warning, even though it is not meant for them. The ones close to him look away, hiding their faces. Rakh continues to stare up at the man. Refusing to budge.

"I am looking for..."

Before Rakh could finish whatever, he was going to say, a huge ~~veuxj qlkk dwkk ib gua gwls.~~

If you did not believe me till now, then there you have it - Cannot lie even as a joke. Everything must be the absolute truth.

Ever had your pen tell you that you are lying? Well, I have. On more than one occasion.

As such, for posterity's sake, what I was writing above was 'a huge brick wall fell on his head' and what actually happened was that the huge man struck Rakh with a blow so hard it knocked him out cold, or worse.

I don't know what exactly, since I can no longer Connect to Rakh's Thread. Hopefully, the blow has not killed him, I was just starting to warm up to him. Time for another break I suppose. Maybe I will look at one of those untouched-forever books. Who knows, maybe I will figure out your interest in reading this book.

Chapter 7

Thread: Unknown

Location: Unknown

Here's an occurrence rarely seen. Another glowing Thread. Inside Svarka itself. Finding two distinct Threads in such proximity to each other. It's unprecedented. This second Thread though. It feels different. Rather than the prismatic glow falling off the Thread, it — it appears to be a void instead. A void in the tapestry. A bizarre characteristic. First recorded by the last Chronicler. How ironic.

Threads connect me to a person and as soon as I Connect to them, I know their identity and the location where they are at the moment.

This thread however has nothing. The location is unrecognisable. Stranger still, I am not tethered to the Thread's source either.

There is a thick mist covering everything. All I can make out is the silhouette of a small village in the distance. It is eerie the way the village is — just there.

Right in the middle of nowhere. Unconnected. Isolated. No roads. No trails. No trees or fields nearby!

Nothing!

I continue moving towards the village. Something is amiss. It should be peak afternoon. The sun should be overhead, shining bright red through Sukarsha. But it's much too dark. Even considering the mist, it's too dark. At least the faint red glow of Sukarsha should be visible. But it's not.

Perhaps I lost track of time inside the cavern. It could be sometime around dusk or dawn.

But it's not just the light. Everything about this place has me on edge. It's all wrong. The air is still, but I feel a chill in my bones. There are no sounds other than the crunching of dry leaves below my feet.

Dry leaves from where? Which tree?

Should I return? Interrupt the Connection?

No. That will be unnecessary.

During a Connection or Delve, I am not subject to harm. I am but an incorporeal observer. Not entirely here. I cannot interact with anything, and neither can anything interact with me.

It's just my mind creating fear in the face of something unknown.

I continue my approach towards the village with caution. It looks like it is less than an hour's walk away. There is no cover to hide one's approach. But I do not need any. I am incorporeal. Not here.

I see strange shapes moving in the mist. Flitting across my periphery. However, as soon as I turn towards them, they are gone. There is a constant wind now. But everything is still silent. Everything but my footsteps.

My courage wanes with every passing moment, I stop. A short distance away from the village.

Perhaps I *should* return to where I Connected to this Thread. I might pick up a clue as to what is going on here.

I was too hasty. I should have observed more before moving to the village.

I am afraid of what is happening here. This silence is gnawing at me. Why am I not tethered to the Thread's Source? What are these shapes that are flitting about in this strange mist?

As I am walking backwards, I abruptly hit something behind me. I am frozen with an overwhelming sense of dread, unable to move or turn. I feel a warm breath down the back of my head. A hissing sound follows each breath. I stand still, waiting for whatever it was that stood behind me to make its move, but it never does. After what feels like an eternity, I pluck the courage to turn around.

I turn my head to witness a monstrosity. Almost human. The size of a full-grown adult. But its frame spindly. Nothing but bones, almost skeletal. Its body is covered in a kind of black liquid that pools at its feet constantly. Its head is where all semblance of humanity vanishes. It — is that of a giant hooded snake, constantly lashing out its tongue.

But it ignores me. It has no interest in me. It is staring with singular focus towards the village.

It takes a step forward, gently brushing me aside. As it continues its walk towards the village, I stay rooted in place. I do not want to do anything to grab this horrendous creature's interest.

I am waiting for it to put some distance between us.

I turn and run back to try and find the place where the Connection had brought me first. But it all looks the same. I don't know where I am. I am afraid.

I need to leave this place!

Why can't I leave this Thread?

I keep running, but everything looks the same. I have no sense of distance. No landmarks to follow. Except for that village and the approaching creature. But no matter which direction I run in, everything I turn, they are still there. Still the same distance.

I cannot find a way to leave this place. The mist — seems to have thickened too. In all directions except for one. What little I could see is now hidden, except for — them. But the wind, it blows harder now. It lashes at my skin. Making me shiver. But still silent. Everything is silent. Except for the crunching of the leaves below my feet.

The crunching...

of leaves...

I look down. I can see my feet. I raise my hands. These are my hands. Scars and all.

No!

No!

How? I am not here physically. I am in a cavern far away from here. The chill in the wind, the leaves crunching under my weight. It's all impossible. The Chronicle does not work this way. I. am. not Here.

Before I can piece together what is happening, the ground shifts below my feet.

I am standing facing the village entrance. Its abnormally large gates loom over me. On either side, the boundary of the village extends to the horizon. Sharply pointed stakes are dug into the ground. All the tops of the wooden posts are chiselled to a point. What little I can see inside the village; the houses are adorned in a similar fashion. Pointed sticks jutting out from wherever possible.

The snake-headed creature is there next to me. Still paying me no heed. Unmoving. Even the tongue has ceased its continuous movement. It stands there in anticipation.

Without warning, the gates of the village open up with a deafening creek. The force pushes me back several steps. There is movement inside the village. But nothing human. Black creatures with no discernible faces. They shamble in unison — limbs crooked and bent in all the wrong directions. As much as I want to run, I cannot. My legs rooted in place. I cannot turn away.

A sudden wail fills the air. The snake-headed creature has raised its hands to the skies and is letting out the unnatural cry. The village creatures turn towards it. Even without faces, it is apparent that they stare at the wailing snake-headed creature. They do not move any further. Standing there intently focused on the creature.

As abruptly as it had started, the snake creature stops its cry. Now looking straight at the village creatures as if taunting them. Within moments everything in the village catches fire. The entire village. Covered in large flames.

In the light of the flames, I see the creatures clearly. They are indeed humans. Their skin melted and charred black. Bodies bent and broken. They were tortured and burnt alive. I try to look away but I cannot. I am forced to look at the horror.

My thoughts, they race through my past. Trying to justify these events. But they fail. The Chronicle. The Threads. They offer no solace at this time.

The snake-headed creature steps towards the undead villagers. With each step it takes, the creatures get more animated. They flail their arms towards the serpent. Swiping at the air but despite their posturing, none of them take a step forward to meet the serpent creature. The serpent creature too stops right at the village gates. Not stepping over the threshold into the village.

All this while I stand fixated. Unable to move away. Somehow caught in the middle of this horrific confrontation.

As my panic rises, I notice a subtle movement in the undead. They melt and start coalescing together. Into a single shapeless mass of burnt flesh. Larger and larger until all the undead have coalesced into a single towering mass.

Suddenly a gaping maw opens up in the mass. The undead mass starts slithering forward as the maw opens wide. Wider and wider, until it stretches from the ground to the top of the towering gates of the village. Within the maw is a blackness. A deep blackness. And from its unfathomable depth comes a blood-curdling scream. Hundreds, no, thousands of voices crying out in unison.

Uttering a single word, laced in pain and torment.

"Murderer!"

Even the mists seem to be echoing the word over and over. The noise deafening. I hold my hands to my ears and look on as the slithering mass lurches forward. The towering monstrosity widens its maw and smashes it down on top of me with great force. I am sucked in without so much as a struggle.

I am floating. In an infinite nothingness. There is a constant murmur around me. Thousands of voices speaking a single word over and over. I cannot hear it clearly.

Argh! Pain!

I am being ripped apart by thousands of hands. They grab and pull at me from all directions. Scratching, clawing, tearing me apart.

Pain. There is nothing but unending pain. I am broken into a thousand pieces, yet the pain endures.

> Wait. There is another voice here. In the infinite blackness. Louder than the murmur.

> I can hear it screaming in pain too. Shouting into the void.

Destruction!

Fire!

My redemption!

Destruction!

It burns! Everything shall burn.

You! Who are you?

I have its attention now.

It knows I am here. But — but it cannot.

What are you doing here?

The screaming voice. It is taking control.
Deafening.

I can't...

This is my nightmare! You. Do. Not. Belong. Here.

There is a menace in the voice.

But this isn't...

Leave me!

How are...

Leave!

Anger. Frustration. Finality.

Let me go! Let... me...go...

Chapter 8

I have been out for several hours. I assume. It's difficult to keep track of time accurately inside an underground cavern. For now, all my time keeping is through the Connections.

The Connections.

My avenue to escape the dread I continue to experience in my own skin.

Snatched away.

Must I lose it all? Piece by piece by piece.

What I would give to not be a Krihaani. Living in ignorant bliss. Praying to the gods. Blessing Sukarsha. Going about my day. Playing with others my age. Never questioning the *truths* accepted by all as facts. And then. Let the end wash over me in an instant. Never realising what happened.

Probably nothing. If I never knew this life, I would not know what I miss.

But I do. I know so much. Yet in the grand scheme of things there is still so much more to know.

Would I — the I that exists now — truly give up all this?

We will never know until such an opportunity arises. Trust me in this. Connecting to others; it gives you an insight you seldom gain while living in your own singular mind. Promises. words given, they are all meaningless, until an opportunity to break them truly occurs. Everyone, in their vision of themselves, is righteous. Until the choice presents itself. That — is when the factual character of a person shines. In the face of temptation.

Until I truly get the chance to leave this life behind, I myself do not know what I would do.

So, despite the shock that was the last Connection. Despite the fear that still makes me tremble. I will continue my duty. In the face of the impossible, I debate, I conjecture, but I continue.

Perhaps it was the wild magic seeping through the barrier. Sukarsha has been weakening much, much, longer than I have been alive. But then, Rakh's Thread is just as close to the edge as this Thread was.

I suppose you and I will uncover the truth when we uncover it. I will add this to the list of mysteries I need to solve before Sukarsha completely fails.

Or, maybe, I should take my experience in that Thread and give myself a sliver of hope.

Though this latest Thread has shaken me to the core. I did survive it. Despite never encountering or hearing about something similar. Perhaps, I will survive my first apocalypse too.

Somehow, I hope.

Fleeting, false hope.

Odd... or a rather disturbing observation.

The last Thread flared only when Rakh was unconscious. Now that he is conscious again, the new Thread has subsided. It's still active, and I will avoid Connecting to it without knowing more, but I think it's more than a mere coincidence. The two Threads are related somehow. But for now, I return to the observational safety of Rakh's Thread.

Chapter 9

Thread: Rakh

Location: Svarka

Thank Sukarsha, he is alive!

The end of the world would be quite dreary without him gallivanting around.

I guess a thick skull has its unique advantages.

Rakh is looking around, his vision is a little blurry. The room he is in is very dark. It is hard to tell whether it is day or night outside. There is a tiny sliver of light coming through a crack a few steps in front of him. Possibly a door, or a large window.

Were it not for this sliver of light I would have abandoned this Thread without giving it a second thought.

Rakh tries to stand up, but he jerks back. He is secured to something. His struggle to break free makes a small ruckus. Moments later the sliver of light widens as a door opens outwards, and the silhouette of a man can be seen holding it open. It's the same person who had gone in to inform the wall-like man in the inn.

Seems we will be seeing more of that giant of a person again. I should Glean him when Rakh sees him next.

Rakh squints at the doorway, the sudden light piercing his eyes, adjusted to the darkness of the room.

“He is awake Rubio,” the man yells to someone from the door.

The large man walks in through the door momentarily. The other man lights a torch near the door and steps back to right outside the door.

“Leave”, Rubio says in a hard voice.

“M-m-me, Rubio?”

“Yes, Rezik. You.”

Rubio casts a glance back towards Rezik. His eyebrows raised. Glowering at him.

“Unless you failed to tie down this fool properly, I don’t see who else would I command to leave this room...”

“N-no, Rubio, I mean yes. I mean you know what the Crows will say if I leave you alone with him!” He stammers out, “I can’t face their anger again!”

“Unless you have a death wish, I am sure you are going to keep your mouth shut about what’s happening here.”

Rubio turns to face Rezik. His frame entirely covering the cowering form of Rezik. Rubio slowly walks forward as Rezik stumbles backwards out of the room.

Rubio gives a mirthless smile as he closes the door on Rezik's face, "And since you are such a loyal servant. I will not mention your lapse to the Crows either. Now leave."

Sounds of Rezik scampering away can be heard through the door.

Satisfied that they are alone, Rubio moves to Rakh. A cruel smile forms as he looks down at his prisoner.

"Now, Rakh. You and I have long unfinished business. And this time none of your precious Talons are around to save you."

Rubio pulls out a sword from his side. And raises it over his head.

> It is a sword, but in the hands of this large man, it appears to be no larger than a dagger.

He brings down the blade and with a single blow breaks the pole to which Rakh is tied.

"Would have been easier to just untie the knots. You don't have to swing around that sword of yours every chance you get", Rakh says with a smile on his face. Rubbing his wrists as the chains fall off.

"Bah! This bitty thing? I will show you what a real sword looks like one of these days," Rubio says with a wave of his hands.

> I am utterly confused here. Flummoxed even. I was completely expecting Rakh to at least get a grievous wound.
>
> Wrong again. Twice in as many days! I would have lost a fortune if I were playing a game of Foretelling right now. Did not expect Rubio to know this man.
>
> Speaking of Rubio, I just realised that I did not introduce him to you after the Glean.

Name: Rubio Talsar

Rank: Hoarder

Association: Murder

> Yes, the group calls themselves Murder. No, they do not commit murder. They have their hold on all sorts of crime except murder as far as our records go. I guess they just wanted to have a scary name for themselves.
>
> Okay, with introductions out of the way. Back to the source of my utter confusion!
>
> They are hugging now. Or at least Rubio would call this a hug. Rakh might be feeling a rib or two of his breaking right about now.

"How have you been you hound?" Rubio bellows out.

“It has been years since you last visited these parts. And this time you don’t even have Zirsa with you. How is that angry young child?”

“I would love to answer you once I can breathe”, Rakh grunts, still trapped in Rubio’s ‘hug’

Rubio quickly let’s go of him and gives him a friendly smack on his shoulders.

“Careful. I am still recovering from your previous punch,” Rakh says rubbing his chin. “You did not have to hit that hard. I think you loosened one of my teeth.”

Rubio gives a sheepish grin.

“Bah! Stop whining so much. You know I had to make it look good.”

He looks around as if the walls might have ears, and lowers his voice, “If word spread that a Talon was all chummy with me, the Murder would kick me out. Can’t risk that.”

He pauses for a moment, before a satisfied smile appears on his face, “Besides. Don’t forget our last bout. I owe you for all the coins you made me lose.”

“Didn’t realise the mighty Korinshan general Rubio was afraid of the Crows,” Rakh teases with a sly grin on his face.

"Afraid? Sukarsha fall now! I really did hit you too hard if your head is now filled with such nonsense," Rubio says with mock outrage, "You know why I have to stay in Svarka. And being a part of one of the two big gangs is the only way I can fulfil my mission without constantly having to watch my back."

"The Murders, despite their ridiculous name, are the lesser of two evils in Svarka," Rubio adds with a sheepish expression. Wanting to somehow justify his association with the Murder to Rakh.

"Yes. Yes. No need to get so flustered. I know why you are here," Rakh replies solemnly, "part of the reason I came looking for you."

Rakh pauses for a moment and continues, "I am afraid, I have some bad news."

Rubio quickly raises his finger to his lips to instruct Rakh to go silent. He quickly steps towards the door and opens it in a quick motion.

Rezik falls over into the room as the door is suddenly pulled away.

"Hello again Rezik," Rubio says with an edge to his voice.

"Seeing as you had a difficult time hearing my instructions, I will assume you had a much harder time listening in on my conversation through this very thick door," he says while pointing to the altogether flimsy door he held open.

"What? I can't hear you! It's those cursed musicians. So loud. C... can't hear anything for days after listening to their din", Rezik stammered out in a single breath, still on the floor on all fours.

Rubio gives a curt nod to Rezik and points him to the exit. His eyes look angry enough to burn holes through stones.

Rezik scurries away, not even trying to stand up before he is a good distance away from Rubio. Rubio looks out the door to make sure Rezik is gone and turns back to see Rakh's questioning expression.

"Ignore him," Rubio says with a wave of his hand, "He is a spineless coward. He wouldn't dare speak of this to anyone. Can't risk anyone thinking that he was a part of this in any manner"

"You know best," Rakh replies with a shrug. "Either way, I will be gone long before he has a chance to do any real damage."

"No time to waste then I suppose. Let's talk business. But not here," Rubio says with caution and continues, "There are others like Rezik around who just might have enough initiative to make trouble for us."

He takes a moment to think and comes to a decision.

“Meet me at my hideaway near the market district. It’s the only one with Korinshan colours. It’s a risk having a Talon there, but only if you are seen entering through the front door.

“Not much of a hideaway then, is it? Declaring your old allegiances like that in the open. Might as well put a banner on top with your name too,” Rakh says with a smirk.

Rubio lets out a chuckle and points Rakh towards a Korinshan flag at the back of the room.

“No one cares here. As long as you are not a Talon. Or any kind of magic user, really.”

Rakh gives a knowing nod. “Enough chatter then. Time is running short, and I have already lost half a day to your punch. I will meet you at your hideaway in an hour.”

Rubio immediately slips into a business-like demeanour, nods to Rakh, and steps out and closes the door behind him.

“Rot in there you freak!” He shouts from outside the door and moves away.

Inside Rakh gives a quick smile as a familiar portal opens in front of him. He steps in to be immediately transported to the inn's roof. He sets his sights towards the market district and begins carefully making his way there. He cannot be seen. Not in Svarka of all places. The bounties on any Talon alive or dead, especially him, would be enough to bring the whole criminal population of Svarka nipping at his heels. He could not afford the distraction.

> Now you might be wondering how I can know his thoughts with such detail. The truth is I cannot. Not completely. These are more interpretations of his emotions than his actual thoughts. His wariness. His feeling of urgency. And other small hints I could fill an entire volume explaining.
>
> If I could read thoughts, the first thoughts I would read would be of the assaulters of my people. Find out why they did this. What drove them to such cruelty? Such wanton destruction.
>
> I tried, I truly tried. But all I could get was their bloodlust. Nothing but an overwhelming and unfathomable blood lust.

Chapter 10

Let's step away for a bit. I barely managed to keep myself steady through that Connection. The after effects of the void Thread still linger. Let us take the hour to ourselves. I am sure nothing interesting is going to happen.

I would like to get a few details out of the way. Information I want to share, given that you have already read this far. Simply to make Chronicling easier for me. Its tiring trying to not reveal things at the same time as I write. And for better or worse it seems that, for the moment, you are the only companion I can communicate with in any manner. But I must say, I already know that you are a great listener.

But first, something I want to know. How did you obtain this book?

~~*You stole it.*~~ I cannot imagine how boring or academic one must be to steal a history book.

Well, all I can hope for is that my writings have reached someone who will not misuse the knowledge they contain. And all other such writings.

With that out of the way, let me tell you more about the last few days.

Yes. I know, you know, that all Krihaani excluding me were massacred.

But do you realise the enormity and improbability of this event?

We were shrouded in secrecy. Layers and layers of secrecy. Even the foundational concept of our people, the idea that we should exist — has not left Satraksh

The Chronicle itself was born in these caverns. Seeing the entire world from this hidden corner of the world through the Threads.

By the very first Krihaani, the first Grand Chronicler. So strong was his belief, in keeping his mission to record the factual truth a secret, that he used forbidden Halmvar magic to erase his Thread from the fabric of Prathak. All this so that he could be an observer, nothing but an observer. Then there is that legend, that he, voluntarily, erased even his own memories before he established the order of the Chroniclers.

But I only trust the written word of the Chronicle. Anything else can be manipulated.

Now, you might think of this secrecy, our way of life, as too extreme. But the first Grand Chronicler, and all those who followed, knew that if word about the Chronicle's existence ever got out, there would be untold chaos. No living being is capable of confronting the absolute truth. They would rather live with half-truths and secrets than face the absolute unadulterated truth. It would shatter their sense of self.

All their faults and all their mistakes, their secrets, and shrouded actions. All laid bare for the world to see?

How do you think the peaceful Barani would have reacted if they knew about the hidden wars their council had constantly waged for hundreds of years?

Or coming to recent times, if the Sorni realised that the floods that destroyed multiple towns in their Protectorate were caused by their benevolent neighbours the Korinshan?

With anger. With an overwhelming feeling of betrayal. Utter. Chaos.

So as to prevent such outcomes, the Krihaani were forbidden to leave these caverns and the surrounding grove. None could leave and none could enter. Amongst our protection, the foremost was our inaccessible location. To this day, the closest village is a hundred miles away as a bird flies. Even for reaching the entrance one would have to travel through thick jungles and, rivers so dangerous, only someone foolish or desperate would attempt them.

Or, perhaps, know of the prize at the end of the journey.

If by a stroke of great luck, someone did reach the entrance, mechanical barriers, blended into the natural scenery, would bar their way. The path through known to none but the current Grand Chronicler.

And then came the final defence. The strongest, yet the simplest of shields. A dome manifested just beyond the boundary of Satraksh and part of the surrounding grove. A dome that anyone could walk through, anytime. However, the dome exacted a price to allow passage. The person crossing would lose all memory of the side they crossed from. Walk in to Satraksh and lose all memory of the outside world. Walk out of Satraksh and lose all memory of Satraksh itself.

This simple but powerful spell protected us for centuries — until it didn't.

It failed us. It failed my family. My people. After thousands of years. of what I can now surmise as pure luck, our protections failed us. And now, all that remains are these innumerable volumes of the Chronicle and me in the endless darkness. A clueless child, pretending to be a Chronicler. A Grand

Chronicler at that. Pretending to be someone who can live up to the legacy of my predecessors.

Well, time to pretend some more.

Chapter 11

Thread: Rakh

Location: Rubio's Den

Rakh is seated at a table in a nondescript room. Rubio is pouring out a drink in to two mugs for them.

"Here. Now tell me, what matter has forced the mighty Rakh to grace our little hell away from home," Rubio teases Rakh, as he sets the bottle down and takes a seat across the table from him.

"Something that could very well spell the end of Svarka," Rakh replies solemnly, and gulps from his mug. He mutters something rude about the flavour.

> Oh! Ho! It seems that he can be quite colourful with his language. I choose to not write it down here. After all, I don't know if you are old enough for colourful language such as this. I know I am not.

Rubio rolls his eyes as he lifts his head upwards, "Ever the Talon. Stop being cryptic and melodramatic. Out with it!"

"The Eyes have discovered two new Focus right here in Svarka. And they seem to be moving around."

Rubio scoffs in disbelief. His brows drawn together. His jovial smile replaced with a slight frown.

"You," Rubio speaks loudly, pointing a finger at Rakh, "You personally led a team of Talons across Sukarsha's borders. You scoured for every infernal artefact, focus and whatever else you Slingers like to use."

Rakh sits calmly. Not responding or reacting to Rubio's sudden outburst.

"What you say is impossible," Rubio slams his mug on the table, the drink splashing out. Some of it lands on Rakh.

"Yes," Rakh nods in acknowledgement as he wipes the drink of his face, "It should be impossible."

Opposite to him, Rubio is still staring at Rakh. Not letting himself simmer down. He waves off Rakh's words and looks away. Mumbling under his breath, "I wish I could get rid of all you Slingers."

A sad smile forms on Rakh's face. He gives a slight nod.

"I agree, Slingers have no place in this world," Rakh says in a soft voice.

Rubio jerks up, upon realising that Rakh had heard his words. His angry demeanour, suddenly melting away. He opens his mouth to say something, but Rakh calmly raises a hand to stop him.

"You don't need to explain yourself to me. I know why you feel this way," Rakh says. His voice filled with empathy. He stares in to the distance as he continues talking, "I could tell you exactly how to get rid of the Slingers. Sukarsha save me, I could tell you how to get rid of all magic."

Rakh pauses. His eyes focus back on Rubio, still smiling, "But it is beyond the power of ones such as you and me to accomplish that task. We — we do not have the willpower needed."

> It sounds impossible. If something like this exists, I am sure the Krihaani would have recorded it. Is he lying to give his friend hope? Or — Rakh has knowledge that even the Krihaani do not possess?

Rubio gives a slow nod at Rakh's words. While still not in the jovial mood he was in a short while ago, he has calmed down. He shuffles in place shaking his head while he searches for words.

"Look Rakh, you have been a friend since the day we met. But I cannot bring myself to ignore all the harm your magic has done."

Rubio stops himself. He straightens and takes a deep breath. He raises both his hands in forgiveness.

“Not *your* magic. But you — you know,” he manages to say.

Rakh nods in understanding, “I know Rubio. Why do you think the Talons have spent the last thousands of years confiscating these items.”

A sudden hint of distress passes over Rakh’s face. He closes his eyes as he rubs his left temple with his fingers.

“Something has started awakening them with greater frequency than we have ever seen.” His voice laced with exhaustion and worry. “The Eyes keep discovering a new one every few days.”

“Days,” Rakh says slowly. His façade of calm and strength lost, he slumps into his chair. “I have not rested in months. None of the Talons have.”

Rakh pauses to take another gulp of his mug. He twists his nose

“We cannot let anyone get a hold of these new Focus. A powerful Artefact or a Focus in the wrong hands would only add fuel to the hatred we already face. Give the Triumvirate a reason to renege on the tenuous peace Zirsa brokered with them.”

Another sip, another spattering of colourful language.

"No wonder you are always in such a foul mood. You'd get more taste from boiled water than this excuse of a drink!"

The sullen mood in the room suddenly disappears as Rubio lets out a bellowing laugh. Regaining his composure, Rakh gives himself permission for a toothy smile.

"Let's not deviate further. We are on borrowed time," Rakh says as he pushes away the half-filled mug.

Rubio nods in agreement.

"Agreed. You know I would not be so angry if it weren't — well now it is the Focus, but you are here to take care of that, so —" Rubio shrugs as he waves off his concerns about the Focus. "But I am already dealing with that Nirdak..."

Rakh leans forward abruptly, "Nirdak? Here?"

It took a moment for Rubio to realise Rakh's outburst. His eyes widen, jaw hanging loose.

"I am a *fool*! That — that should have been the first thing I told you," Rubio jumps up from his chair and starts pacing around.

Rakh gestures his friend to be calm, "All is not lost Rubio. I can still sense the Focus. He is still in Svarka."

Rubio stops and looks at Rakh. Nodding quickly, he takes a deep breath and sits back down at the table.

Rakh continues, "It must be someone low on their totem pole. Otherwise, they would be long gone. Either that or they are trying to figure out the nature of the Focus before risking a journey across the wild lands."

"Both scenarios are to my benefit." he adds with a measure of hope in his voice.

"I should have known. I should've never trusted that one-eyed crook. That's the last time I trust a lead from one of them. Bah!" Rubio slams his fist onto the table again. This time with enough force to splinter off part of it.

"A lead?" Rakh asks inquisitively.

"A man named Sunten...."

> That name. It has a ring of familiarity to it. A sense of dread — and solidarity. I must find out more about this person. No time to get distracted.

"...all three of them are somewhere in the market district itself. I wanted it to be the truth!" Rubio exclaims in frustration. "But I see now that he used my reputation to gain an advantage while he searched for the Focus," he continues while pacing around the room.

> When did he get up? How — What did I miss? I said no distractions!

Rakh looks out the window and nods. "It will be dusk soon. By your account, he should be out hunting for marks soon enough. Good time for me to capture him."

Rubio looks to Rakh and nods, "Yes. Get him."

"And once you have your Focus, you bring him to me so that I can squeeze the life out of that duplicitous crook myself," Rubio says while looking down and making a wringing action with his hands.

"Even Yapran himself will be afraid of showing his face in Svarka after I am through with that wretch Sunten," he finishes with a sneer on his face.

"Peace my friend. Let's not jump to conclusions. May be, he is indeed telling the truth," Rakh says putting a hand on Rubio's shoulder.

"Whatever be the reason for his presence here, be assured that I will get to the bottom of it. Let them deal with Rakh first. Before they must face the wrath of the legendary Rubio," Rakh said with a smile.

"You are a good friend Rakh," Rubio says, smiling ear to ear at the compliment.

“I will wait here till I get word of your success. If you need any assistance, look for the guard with Korinshan colours on their lapels. They have my trust. But do not let anyone see you use your Focus. Svarka is much more tolerant than the inner kingdoms, but you cannot be careless.”

Rakh nods. He turns towards the window. A portal appears and Rakh steps through to the roof of the hideaway. As the portal closes a faint curse is heard from the other side, “Right on my rooftop? Bah!”

Chapter 12

No! No breaks this time. You can satiate your ugly hunger about my tragic story another time. I have an uncanny feeling that this is important.

The pulse of the Threads grows stronger.

Chapter 13

I know I said no matter what, I would stay Connected. But this is ridiculous.

Rakh has been standing on the top of this building overlooking the market for two whole hours. He has not moved an inch in all this time.

I even had time to attend a nature's call. In complete darkness. Do you know how difficult it is to find a proper place to relieve yourself in complete darkness?

If I had known he was going to stay still for so long, I would have taken the time to cross off a Delve or two from my ever growing list. Or find more pertinent information about my current situation. Or perhaps replenish my provisions.

What an utter waste of my precious time.

Rakh sharply turns his head to look towards the food traders in the market district.

Finally!

Rakh's vantage gives him a bird's eye view of almost all of the market.

A hobbled-together group of merchants and traders that have taken over the entirety of the open space between the two sections of Svarka. The big merchants have built permanent structures to house and sell their goods, but most are in makeshift structures. Mostly four poles and a canvas roof. The market is divided into clear sections. Merchants of specific categories clustered together. However, no two merchants deal in the same goods. There are traders dealing in multiple types of goods. But no one is selling anything that another merchant is selling.

> Quite a unique system I suppose. Monopolies for everyone.

Rakh moves into the alleyways that surround the market. Making his way through them towards the food merchants. Frugally using his Focus to avoid the guard patrols.

He finally pauses in an alley with an opening behind a bread seller's makeshift shed.

There is another man in the alley. He has registered Rakh's presence yet. He moves silently through the alley. Staying the over-growing shadows of twilight. A perfect time for a thief. Enough shadows for them to move through and just enough remnants of daylight that most people do not feel the need to light torches.

The thief quickly grabs two dry pieces of bread from the back of the shop and turns to escape through the alley. He takes a couple of steps and stops right as the last rays of the sun land on his face through a gap in the buildings.

Name: Sunten

Association: None

He is a man in, maybe, his late twenties. Maybe younger. The signs of struggle and abuse, adding a few years to his appearance. He has multiple scars criss-crossing his face. The biggest of which cuts across his right eye. A makeshift patch covers the socket of his right eye. His clothes are covered in grime. He is wearing a loose shirt, covered in patches added over a long time. The trousers are in a similar condition, tied to his waist with a bit of tweed. Looking at his clothes, you could easily tell that he has been living off the streets for quite some time now.

He is frozen in place. Eyes wide in shock. The loafs fall from his trembling hands.

"You! It's you!" he stammers while pointing towards Rakh.

Rakh gives his most confident smile and takes a step towards Sunten. Right as Rakh is about to grab him, Sunten jolts to life and makes a break for a side alley. He takes a few large strides and without stopping looks back to see Rakh simply standing there. Without turning, he takes a sharp turn into another alley.

Rakh uses his Focus to jump to a location in front of Sunten, who at once crashes into Rakh with force. Unmoved, Rakh tries to grab hold of Sunten, who pushes back with his leg and in a quick recovery starts running away again. Another turn and he once more finds Rakh standing in front of him with a pitying look on his face. Sunten looks to the sides and makes for another side alley. Another turn later he reaches a wide span in the middle of the alleyways. Multiple alleys branch out from this intersection. But everywhere he turns Rakh is there. Slowly herding him towards the centre of the span.

Sunten is sweating profusely now. His breathing laboured. He raises his hands in defence, waving them wildly. Between gasps of air, he yells out, “Let me go. I am sorry. I did not mean for it to happen. Let me go. Please!”

Rakh continues to advance towards Sunten. His lips turned in a sneer. His nostrils flared. He speaks in a voice with a hard edge to it, “You... must be Sunten.”

As soon as he hears his name, Sunten loses all control. In a desperate move, he takes a handful of dirt from the ground and throws it at Rakh. Expecting it to distract Rakh, Sunten makes a quick turn and starts to run. Only to run headlong into Rakh. Seeing him up close again is the final straw for Sunten. He collapses and goes catatonic.

Rakh takes a step forward and grabs hold of Sunten's collar and shakes him. Suddenly a huge rock flies into his peripheral vision. His quick reflexes allow him to narrowly dodge it, but he isn't able to escape the hit of the second smaller rock, which hits him squarely on the back of his head.

Suddenly a voice rings out in the alley.

"Leave him alone!"

A child's voice.

> Yes, a child's voice. Not much of a non-child myself but I can still call a child a child. No rules against that. You don't have to find it funny when I call someone a child.

Rakh looks around to find the source of the sound. He holds on to Sunten's collar, not wanting to let go of his quarry under any circumstances. Another rock flies towards him. This time he is ready and able to track its trajectory from the top of a small house to his left.

He turns and looks up to see two children standing on the corner of the roof.

"I said, Let. Him. Go!", the elder of the two yells at Rakh through gritted teeth. A girl. Perhaps ten or twelve. There is a boy there too. Smaller by a year, perhaps, two. He stands behind the girl. The fear on his face undercutting his combative stance.

Rakh stares at the two children. Stunned to silence. Then breaks out in a hollow laugh. He looks back at Sunten and shakes him hard again.

"This is what the Nirdak have stooped to now? Using images of children?" There is an edge to his voice. "If you thought you were in trouble before, you have no idea what I am going to do to you now. You should have known better than to use *their* images to try and escape."

Rakh swings his hand across Sunten's face. Punching him hard. The blow makes a shallow cut across his cheeks which starts bleeding.

Multiple rocks fly towards Rakh. This time joined by multiple large spinehead quills.

> Spinehead quills?! How in Jvala's name? In the middle of Svarka? Things cannot get any weirder.

One of the quills cuts across his hand. Rakh smarts in pain and, pulls away from Sunten and turns back towards the two children.

He looks on in shock.

Me too. I am looking in shock too. I am stupefied. It's a word I read in one of our older volumes and I am it. Remember the time I said things can't get any weirder? Two sentences ago. Well, they just got weirder.

Chapter 14

In my state of utter shock, I have made an error. You know the void Thread I Connected to, the one which caused me immense pain?

Exactly. That one.

I accidentally broke my Connection to Rakh's Thread and Connected to it. Although, it no longer manifested as a void since Rakh had gained consciousness in Rubio's inn, I was still avoiding it.

You might be confused as to how I could make such a mistake. Let me tell you something — I would rather not say. You have enough information about the Chronicle and Threads. You do not need more. Think of it as a mystery that you will try to solve by yourself. But never will.

For now, the important thing is that I pulled at that Thread again. However, to my utter shock, magnified by my previous state of shock, the Thread belongs to Sunten. Do not ask me how. I am simply not going to ask questions I cannot get answers to from now on. None at all. Only focus on what I need to do.

Do you want a bit of good news too? There is no pain this time. No horrific village surrounded by mists and no serpent-headed monster either. No screaming voices and no one trying to take control either.

Now, you must be thinking that I went out of my way to say that there is good news. Which means there is bad news too.

You are correct. You have an uncanny tendency to be correct.

Moving on. Bad news. I cannot see anything going on around me. No, it's not a fault with the Connection. It is Sunten and well, Rakh is partly to blame. Mostly to blame. His hard blow mere moments ago swung Sunten face-down in the dirt. The Connection allows me to enhance what I see or hear, but it cannot allow me to sense what the Thread Source cannot sense at all. Changing the Thread immediately is not possible either. Must wait for two full turns of the hourglass before I can pick up the same Thread again.

Jvala take whoever manifested these arbitrary rules.

So back to our shocking event. I will quickly describe what I saw before I bring you back to what's happening in the narrow alleys of Svarka.

Chapter 15

Thread: Sunten

Location: Svarka

I saw the elder of the two children, the girl, float off the roof of the house on top of a miniature whirlwind. And the boy transformed into a red hawk and was flying down towards Rakh. I have a giant record of what magic is possible in today's age. Neither of these powers are present there. And children doing any magic whatsoever is rare too.

> That is when I accidentally Connected on Sunten's Thread and now, all I can tell you is what I can hear or feel through Sunten.

"Get back from him! How dare you hit our brother!" The girl says. (Presumably to Rakh)

"Yes, stay away. Or...or I will stomp you with an elephant's foot." The boy.

A slight shudder goes through the ground as he says this.

Rakh is uncharacteristically silent so far. I can't hear or sense any movement from him.

Pebbles crunch under the footsteps of a large boot. Rakh is moving towards Sunten again.

"You better not touch him again! You have hurt him so much already! You are a bad man!" an almost crying voice says. Could be either of the children.

"What? Bad? Me?" Rakh says with incredulity.

"I am not a bad man. He is!" he adds petulantly.

> A good old "No him" response. Very effective in some circles.

Suddenly Sunten is lifted off the ground. He is turned around to face Rakh.

> Finally. Even though the presence of the other senses partly alleviated my panic, the darkness was weighing heavy on me. Both because of the void Thread and my immediate physical surroundings.

Rakh has a fire in his eyes. His glare could melt metal. Both his hands grab Sunten's collar. His teeth bared. There is something primal in his anger.

"You gave the Focus to them?" He yells out at a still catatonic Sunten, "Too afraid to try them on yourself? Should not expect anything from you cowardly Nirdak," Rakh spits out.

At the mention of the Nirdak, a slight shudder goes through Sunten. But he still does not make any movement. Rakh lets him go and he falls in a crouch. Rakh turns to the children. Both of them are covered in streaks of dirt. They look like they have not eaten for days. Sunken eyes and all skin and bones. Their clothes are tattered like Sunten's, with crude patchwork repair all over. But that is where the similarity ends. Where Sunten has blunt facial features and a broad frame, the two children are completely different. Both have sharp facial features and lean figures. Where Sunten has light brown hair, both children have jet-black hair. Their faces are similar enough to show that they are related to each other. But certainly not to Sunten.

They are standing a few steps away from Rakh. Eyeing him warily. Suddenly a rock flies towards Rakh from his side. He reflexively catches it in his hand without taking his eyes off the children. The stone suddenly catches fire. Rakh lets it go with a yelp. This brings out a smile on the girl's face.

"Serves you right!" she says sticking her nose up. Rakh stares at her and shifts his gaze to the boy. Finding Rakh's attention on him, the boy suddenly makes a face.

How childish!

Rakh looks at the boy and suddenly breaks out in a smile.

“Don’t you smile at us after you hurt our brother! I will —” The girl looks around, trying to think off a threat.

“I will break all the bones in your body!” she yells finally with the confidence only a child can muster in such a situation.

Rakh takes on a sombre expression again. “Now I have had enough of your petulance!” he says in a raised voice. Frustration laces his voice. He is only trying to protect these children.

“I am only trying to save you from whatever dangerous object this spineless coward has given you!”

The girl makes a sudden move towards Rakh, her left hand covered in flame. But before she could take a step forward, Rakh flashes behind the two children.

He immediately picks them up by the collars. Both of them start struggling to get out of his hold. The boy suddenly starts making wild transformations. Claws on one hand, bird’s talons on another! Fur and fangs on his face! Instant later all gone and a prehensile tail shows up trying to swat at Rakh! The girl on the other side tries to slash at him with her fire hand, but his hold is too strong to let her turn and do so. An ice ball springs out of her other hand but in her struggle, she misses Rakh and propels towards Dvija. Only Rakh's timely action saves Dvija from getting hit by the solid ice ball.

"Enough!" Rakh yells out in anger. "If you don't stop this foolishness right now, you are going to get hurt!"

"Agni! Dvija! Stop right now!" Sunten's voice rings across the alleyway.

Both the girl and boy immediately stop struggling and look towards Sunten. A great smile crosses their face.

"Sunten! You are okay!" they say in unison. Rakh looks surprised at their sudden change in mannerisms. He turns to Sunten. Eyes narrowed, an eyebrow raised. His control over the children piquing his curiosity.

Sunten raises his hand in surrender and continues to speak, "Let them down, please! They are innocent. They haven't done anything wrong." He looks to the children and in a stern voice reprimands them, "Agni! Dvija! stop this nonsense immediately."

He looks to Rakh again and pleads to him, "We...we will go with you Talon! We will go peacefully. Don't harm them."

The girl gives a curt nod to Rakh as if her acknowledgement was required for any further action. Rakh lets both down. Sunten slowly stands with great difficulty. The chase and the ensuing confrontation have left him weak.

“Lead the way, Talon. We will follow.”

“Oh no, Nirdak! Not like this. These children trust you out of innocence, I don’t. I am not taking anyone anywhere until I have the Focus in my possession. Sukarsha will fall before I trust a Nirdak.”

Through gritted teeth, with great effort, Sunten speaks up, “I. am. Not. A. Nird...”

He faints before he can complete his sentence.

Time to leave.

Chapter 16

I know it's the end of the world and all. Well, end of the world for me. For you, it has probably already ended.

Either way! End of the world. But do things have to be so...so... *strange* right at the end? All these weird things happening right as the world is ending and no time to actually savour them. Enjoy the weirdness.

I remember when I would spend hours upon hours in the archives. There was an entire section dedicated to unexplained or anomalous records. There was one about the Priest of the Soniras temple. Wars were fought by those who coveted their blessing. But no matter how far we Delved, no one could find the source of their power. Then there was the village of Saranik. That — that was a Knot few dared unravel. Four Threads converged there. And the outcome. It gave nightmares to all those who witnessed those events through the Threads. Just reading those records gave me sleepless nights for months. Then there was the Day of No Deaths, the overnight disappearance of the Tridhak empire, the emergence of the Vah'ron, the Five *Immortal* Guardians. I could go on and on.

No one else would ever visit that section. It was as if — it was made just for me. Surprisingly, the archives themselves were an anomaly for me. I never saw any of the Chroniclers make any attempt to catalogue or organise the archives. Finished volumes would be simply placed in the closes free rack. I myself dropped tens of volumes written by my mother there. And miraculously, in days, weeks during busy times, the volumes would be neatly catalogued and moved into one of the designated sections.

The archives were my favourite place. The quiet, the isolation. All things I yearned for mere days ago. Everything I now despise. Forced upon me by living nightmares.

Enough reminiscing though. I know what you were expecting when you came here. More information about the death of the Krihaani.

Sorry to disappoint, but I have more important things to do. Rakh's and Sunten's are not the only Threads I must follow. They might be the two most important right now, but — there are more Threads that I must follow to fully understand and record the end of the world.

I have already ignored them for too long. The longer I ignore them, the farther I will have to Delve to discover their full extent. Since we cannot Connect to either Rakh or Sunten for some time yet, might as well get one or two of these other Threads out of the way as we can. Think of it as a cleansing Connection. It should allow us to truly enjoy the more captivating events that come with the most important Threads.

Let us Connect to someone with authority. Someone I am sure you already like as much as I do.

Chapter 17

Thread: Zirsa

Location: Vaasat

Zirsa stands on a balcony overlooking the Grove of the Talons. She is admiring the natural beauty of the Grove. She brushes her hand over the balcony handrail. A slight smile forms on her face. She turns to the woman standing behind her in perfect attention, calm and patient. Not uttering a word while Zirsa is deep in thought. The woman is dressed in a formal attire. She wears a long gray skirt and a white blouse. Her hair neatly tied in a bun at the back of her head. She looks to be in her mid-twenties. Almost as tall as Zirsa she looks straight in her eyes.

Zirsa asks her to the balcony. The woman walks over and stands silently. Waiting once more for Zirsa to speak.

"Kintra, do send a letter of appreciation to the builders."

She looks back out to the grove and continues,

“Especially, Prime Builder Wrick. His team never ceases to amaze me. He has managed to mould the forest around us to create all the perks of civilisation without disturbing the life force of the forest itself. Don’t you think so?”

Name: Kintra

Affiliation: Talons of the Firebird

Rank:: Unranked

Kintra nods in acknowledgement and replies, “Certainly Zirsa. I will do so immediately.”

Zirsa raises an eyebrow at Kintra’s cold response, “I know you were born in Vaasat and have grown to see Wrick’s work as commonplace. But I assure you it’s not.”

Unaffected, Kintra gives another nod and attempts to divert Zirsa to the day’s tasks. She is carrying a bundle of paper with her. Separated into smaller groups and tied together with thread. There is a dark envelope at the bottom of the bundle.

“We have a full load today Zirsa,” she says simply.

Zirsa decides not to push further for now and gestures Kintra to lead the way.

They exit the balcony onto a large landing. There are two staircases on either side. Both going down.

Kintra points to the staircase on the left and sighs before speaking.

"We have another intake of refugees today. All commoners," Kintra says with a hint of annoyance in her voice. The first time she has shown emotion in this conversation.

Zirsa starts walking down the stairs as Kintra follows.

"One of them is being particularly difficult. He insists on meeting someone named Sinara."

"Does not sound familiar. Have you looked in the rolls? Perhaps another refugee?", Zirsa suggests.

"I have already asked the Keepers to do so."

"Good, let's go meet these new residents of Vaasat."

They reach the bottom of the staircase and head into a large circular hall in front of them. The hall is similar to the rest of the building. The walls moulded out of living trees. Along the wall, pillars have been formed by the aid of intertwining thick hanging roots together. The floor, the furniture, everything appeared to grow out of the ground and flow back into it. In the middle of the hall surrounded by a dozen Talon guards, a couple dozen people are seated on the ground in various states of exhaustion. There are two families amongst them, with children. The children cry loudly. Likely with hunger. A lone man sits to the side leaning against a pillar. He holds his head in his hands. He is mumbling something to himself over and over.

Zirsa scans the room and turns to Kintra, “I do not see any food or water provided to these refugees. Have they just arrived?”

Without a change in her cold demeanour, Kintra answers, “I did not think it prudent to waste resources on refugees that we might turn away.”

Zirsa takes a sharp breath and tightens her jaw. She clenches her fist. A child’s loud wail interrupts her before she could say anything. She sharply turns away from Kintra to look at the refugees. She gestures one of the guards to come forward.

“See to providing all these refugees with food and water. And make sure everyone — “, Zirsa casts a pointed glance at Kintra.

“*Everyone* knows that this is to be done for all refugees going forward. I need not repeat myself” Zirsa says in a firm voice as she walks away towards the lone man by the pillar.

Behind her Kintra is flustered. Her brows furrowed, she looks at the refugees and back to Zirsa. She does not understand the reason for this sudden reaction from her. She shakes her head and follows Zirsa, to warn her about the troublesome refugee she was approaching.

Zirsa kneels down near the refugee and takes his hands to comfort him. Before she can say anything, the refugee starts speaking loudly, "Sinara! Thank Jvala, I found you. She is awakening."

> Its Ridsan! I did not recognise him through the layers of grime on him. But the voice. Its unmistakable.

Zirsa looks closely at Ridsan. His eyes are glazed over. His iris pale. She slowly nods; understanding his condition.

"I am not Sinara, but I will do my best to help you find her," she says sympathetically.

Kintra watching the interaction so far, interjects, "We believe he may be deaf Zirsa. He has not responded to any of our instructions so far."

Zirsa looks at Kintra, sadness reflecting in her eyes. She nods and turns back to Ridsan. She takes his left hand and holds it palm up in her left hand. With her right hand's index finger, she draws a series of gestures on his palm.

Ridsan takes a sharp breath. And in the next instant starts sobbing. He takes Zirsa's hands to his forehead.

"Thank you! Thank you! I will wait for her here. Thank you!", he says between ragged gasps.

Zirsa pats his shoulder to console him and stands up to leave. Kintra follows behind. Zirsa speaks to the other refugees one after the other. Then instructs the guards to take them all to the Keeper of Records to take down their details. And from there guide them to their assigned shelter.

She tells one of the guards to stay with Ridsan and to immediately let her know if he acts up again. With this Zirsa and Kintra exit the hall.

As they walk through the corridor towards their next destination. The daylight shining through large windows brightens the atmosphere. Here the builders had let their creative side loose. With the presence of natural light, they were able to cover everything but the floor with greenery. Leaves and flowers of various shapes and sizes beautifully adorned along the walls and ceiling. Except for the presence of pillars shaped from tree trunks at regular intervals, everything else was random. Unorganised. Chaotic. Natural. Zirsa, who previously could not help herself from admiring the beauty of a moulded rail, does not cast a look at anything in this corridor. She walks back straight, head raised, and eyes coldly locked at the other end of the corridor. Behind her Kintra outlines the rest of the day for Zirsa. Her meetings with the council. Her debriefing with Suthrin and Donas from their mission.

So on and so forth. Zirsa merely acknowledges with a nod of her head. Not even turning to look at Kintra.

Eventually, Kintra plucks the courage to question the demeanour. Right before they were about to exit the corridor, she stops in place. Takes a deep breath, straightens herself and in a firm voice questions Zirsa, "Have I offended you in some manner Zirsa?"

Zirsa who had not noticed Kintra stopping, pauses mid stride. She turns to face Kintra. A sad smile on her face. She looks around her. As if noticing the beauty for the first time. She turns to Kintra again, "No. Not offended."

Zirsa pauses. Opening and closing her mouth, trying to find the right words to say next.

Kintra to her credit remains motionless.

> She has the patience of a mountain yak. A young impatient yak. But more than what is expected of a common person.

Zirsa finally finds her voice again, "But you have disappointed me today."

Kintra lowers her head. Her grip on the bundle of papers she is holding tightens. Tears well up in her eyes, but she pushes them back. She looks back up when Zirsa starts speaking again.

“You were recently inducted into our order Kintra. I do not expect you to know all about us. But I do expect you to understand why we do what we do.”

Kintra nods her head like a child admonished by their parent for no discernible reason.

> I know that feeling all too well. What I would not do to feel it once more.

Zirsa walks over to a window and beckons Kintra to join her.

She points to a tall tower in the middle of their grove. It is surrounded by four buildings, smaller in size, in each direction. The tower and these buildings, the only things of artificial construction. Made of large quarried stones. They appear to have been part of some kind of fortification in the distant past.

“That is all the Talons had. Eons ago. Before the barrier. Before the Vah’ron Halmvar war. Everything else you see, even where we stand. All were created much later.”

Kintra looks on. She nods knowingly.

Zirsa continues, “In those days, the Talons were celebrated heroes. They were one of four such groups that existed across Prathak. Protecting the lands from threats within and without. This, one of many such fortifications, remained a secret not by design. But by chance. They were not much for record keeping. And Vaasat was never important enough for them for it to be public. With perhaps ten Channelers or Casters at any given time, it could be considered more of an outpost for them"

Kintra begins shuffling in her place. The connections between this history lesson and Zirsa's admonishment, escaping her.

Zirsa looks over with a smile and continues," Don't worry, I will not be giving you an exhaustive history lesson. Your instructors will be doing that. I will skip to the important part."

She walks over to the doors at the end of the corridor and exits to a viewing gallery. Below them the room contains a large round table moulded from the ground. All but one of the ten seats around the table are occupied.

Zirsa speaks in a low voice, "Each one of them, even me and you. All of us were given refuge by the Talons."

Kintra looks unconvinced. She subtly shakes her head. Her brows brought together. She is about to say something, but Zirsa raises her hand to silence her.

"You could say some, like you were born here. However, your parents or grandparents, or one of your ancestors. would have received refuge here.

There are but three Talons alive who can trace their lineage to any of the original Talons."

Kintra nods her head in agreement. Ceding the point she never got to make.

"When Sukarsha was raised, there was chaos. For obvious reasons, the only protectors left were the Talons. We helped the three ruling families to bring order. We were showered with gratitude until the truth was discovered."

> Talons and truth? Hard to imagine. Especially coming from a Zirsa.

"That Sukarsha protects us from raging storms beyond its border. But all they could ascertain was that Channelers and Casters were involved with both the formation of the storms and Sukarsha. No one knows of their true origins."

> I could name a few who do. Or I could have a few days ago. Now I can name one. ~~And know about another~~. Or maybe I do not?

Kintra interjects. Her patience giving out.

"Pardon the interruption Zirsa, but I am well aware of our origins. But how does that affect the unending deluge of refugees who seek our aid? Channelers and Casters, even Slingers and commoners. They drain our resources and put everyone here at risk with their presence. We cannot keep Vaasat a secret if we keep expanding at this rate."

Kintra takes a breath, she spoke louder than she wanted to. Below them those sitting at the table look up. Surprised at the sudden outburst. Zirsa raises her hand towards them to signal her presence. All, but one, nod and go back to studying the reports in front of them. An elderly man continues staring at Zirsa and Kintra. He meets Kintra's eyes in a questioning glance. Kintra shakes her head in response and turns away to look at Zirsa.

"I — I apologise Zirsa for my outburst."

Zirsa smiles and continues, "It is one of you better qualities Kintra. Question authority. Not blindly follow your leader. But that does not exempt you from understanding."

Zirsa turns to a winding staircase that goes down towards the council meeting room. As she walks down, she takes Kintra to her side and says, "We help the refugee because Vaasat is not ours. It was a refuge for us and our ancestors. And that is how it must stay. None of us have the authority to change its nature. A refuge freely given to those in need."

Kintra looks at Zirsa with understanding in her eyes. She vigorously nods her head and smiles at Zirsa.

“Thank you Zirsa. I — I will attempt to keep my mind open towards those that need our aid.”

Zirsa gives a slow nod. They reach the table and Zirsa takes her seat at the only empty chair at the table. Beside her, the elderly man from earlier looks at Kintra. Seeing her smile, he returns it.

Kintra hands over the black envelope, she had been carrying, to Zirsa and leaves the room. There are similar envelopes opened, and their contents taken out in front of the other council members.

Zirsa quickly reads through the first page. A look of concern passes over her face. Her calm demeanour after reconciling with Kintra, replaced by a businesslike attitude.

The other council members share her concern.

The pages in front of her contain reports from the Eyes. They have discovered two new Artefacts in the past two days.

> As I close in from my vantage point to see the details of the report, Zirsa suddenly turns her head to where my vantage point would be if I were physically there.

She moves her eyes around, looking for something that is not there. She narrows her eyes in thought.

Then she tilts her head in the direction of the reports and turns back to them.

> I am intrigued. And a little afraid. This is all very strange. Can she sense me somehow? And if so, is she trying to get me to look at a report? Maybe the magic that protects her identity is allowing her to sense me? But why the gesture towards the report?

She shuffles the pages. First a roughly drawn map showing the locations of the discovered Artefacts. She traces her finger along the map. A village is marked near the first Artefact location. She slowly traces her finger to the next Artefact and then past its location to another village. At the edge of the Torika Null.

> It took me a moment to piece together the meaning of her actions. She was implying something dreadful. Something to be avoided at all costs, but seemingly unavoidable now. Both villages were under the control of the same force. The Nirdak.
>
> But am I imagining that she is trying to share this information with me? What is the use? Not like —

She makes a big show of bringing another page on top. It is a report from one of their undercover agents in Valdas. They mention fearing for their safety and the other Slingers in Valdas.

I have no inkling if all this is the imagination of my tired mind or if this information is being specifically conveyed to me by Zirsa. However, as a Chronicler, I cannot ignore them. While I cannot do anything about the Artefact; being confined in this cavern. I can certainly gather information about the situation in Valdas. And it so happens, a Thread of prominence exists there.

We have a little more than another turn of the hourglass before I will be able to Connect to Rakh's Thread again. Enough to see what new knowledge one Setsek has for us.

Chapter 18

Thread: Setsek

Location: Valdas Castle

Setsek sits cross legged, facing the door of a small cold room. The first moon visible in the small high window behind him. It is late in the night and there are no torches in the room. But the roughly polished gray stones of the room reflect the first moon's light well enough. Setsek, of average height, if not shorter, could probably lie down with his hands and legs outstretched to touch all four walls at once. The only item of comfort in the room was the straw mattress he is kneeling on. Even the clothes on his back are made with a flimsy cloth. Barely able to keep him warm against the bitter cold of the Valdasin winter, if at all.

In any other situation, I would call this a prison cell. But in Valdas, this bordered on luxury. The only *better* room would be reserved for the Commander Superior, and it would be smaller than this. Windowless. And the mattress replaced with a single sheet of cloth made of the same material as Setsek's clothing. Frugality and discomfortiture were signs of strength for the Valdasin.

Maybe I should send out an application to them for grant of citizenship. Given my current circumstances I could probably be elevated to some kind of worshippable status

Setsek fidgets continuously as he rocks back and forth. Clenching and unclenching his fists over and over. He perks up every time a whisper of a sound falls on his ears. But he is not nervous. He is alert, not moving his eyes from the door for an instant. A glint in his eyes. He is taking quick shallow breaths. The corner of his lips upturned. They quiver in anticipation. On the edge of turning into a large smile. He is expecting news. Of the good kind.

It takes around half a turn of the hourglass before a loud scream pierces the thick door.

Without wasting a moment Setsek jumps up, and yank opens the door and steps out. His room is somewhere close to the middle of a long corridor. While the same gray stones have been used to construct the corridor as well, they are dull and unpolished. Sparsely placed torches light the corridor. There are no other doors along the sides. One end branches out to other corridors, and the other on his left exits through a large wooden door.

Right outside Setsek's door is a man on his knees. Head held high, grinning ear to ear. He holds out an unadorned sword with both hands towards Setsek. He is dressed in similar fashion to Setsek. Except for a golden lace that adorns his sleeves. He is several ranks below Setsek in the Valdasin hierarchy.

"Lord Setsek," he says reverently, "it is time."

Even as six men, armed with swords and spears, approach them with caution from both ends of the corridor, Setsek and the kneeling man pay them no heed.

Setsek continues staring at the sword. He closes his eyes for a moment. He takes a deep breath and opens his eyes, followed by a loud hurrah. He gleefully grabs the sword and rushes headlong towards the four men approaching from the exit. Behind him the kneeling man lets out a cry and rushes towards the other two men.

The sound of swords clashing fill the corridor. Both Setsek and his associate are skilled beyond measure. More than I have ever seen. They weave in and out of their adversaries' attacks. Not letting them land a single attack. While every slash of their own swords spilt blood. However, even in their frenzy they attack carefully to avoid any fatal wounds.

> The way they move, their swordplay, there is something familiar about them.

Almost in the blink of an eye they have incapacitated all the attackers. Looking to his aide, Setsek nods in appreciation. He steps over the unconscious bodies of his attackers to rush to the exit door.

Right into the castle's innermost sanctum. Surrounded by high walls the night sky and Sukarsha's dull red glow visible overhead. The first moon has reached its zenith. Soon the second moon will rise.

Hundreds of Valdasin stand silently on the ramparts. Looking down at the events with expressionless eyes. As observers with no stake in the outcome of the events. Dressed in well-made clothes that keep the cold out. A sea of colour contrasted against the dull gray of the castle walls. The commoners of Valdas. Labourers, traders, merchants, service men...

> ...anyone except for those inducted into the Valdasin warrior class. A strange method to enforce equality. Years were spent by Krihaani of philosophical disposition. Debating which part of the Valdasin society was better off. The commoners who have all the resources, or the warriors who hold all the power.
>
> From what I have seen in the past few weeks, the answer is always the ones who hold all the power.

The only entrance or exit to this part of the castle is through the door where Setsek ran in. In front of him a spiral corridor leads away to the centre. Ahead, where the corridor narrows down significantly, stand three others, two female and a male Valdasin. They are dressed like Setsek and his aide. Two of them have silver lacing their arms and one of the females has a bronze lacing. They stand their ground against the onslaught of tens of opponents who are attempting to break through to Setsek.

Setsek gives a rallying cry as his aide next to him rushes to join his fellow combatants.

"Lord Setsek," his aide yells, as he decapacitates another man with his swift attacks, "the second moonrise will be upon us any moment. Leave these insignificant bugs to us. You must push forward and seize this night for our cause"

Setsek nods in appreciation and rushes over to the wall. Using slits made for archers he deftly climbs to the top of the wall. The Valdasin standing at the top make room for him. They offer neither help nor resistance to his actions. He runs along the wall's top to avoid the blockage below. From the walls he can see the central arena. That is his goal. He takes a quick look at the first moon coming down from its peak. He is running out of time. He quickly scans the fight below and the ramparts to determine the fastest way to reach the arena. He runs along the outer edge of the wall. Right where the wall swerves away from the central section of the castle, he makes a long jump to grab a support beam jutting out from the central wall.

> The only other person I would expect to have made that jump would have been Rakh. With the aid of his Focus. Setsek is inhuman.

Setsek climbs over the central wall and jumps into the central arena. In the middle of the arena a bald man stands patiently. He is of similar age to Setsek. Though, where Setsek is lean and muscular, this man is stout. His clothes are flimsy like Setsek's, but he has no shirt on. Naked from the waist up. He is staring at Setsek with anger in his eyes. He stands straight with his fists clenched on his side. His mouth upturned in disgust.

Name: Peksur

Affiliation: Valdas

Rank: Supreme Commander (Warrior Sect)

As Setsek approaches Peksur, he lowers his sword. Giving a curt bow he speaks loud enough for everyone present to hear, "Supreme Commander Peksur, I challenge you to the Trial of the Two Edges. I left my chamber with the rise of Serant, and have reached the arena before Perantes, the second moon has risen above the horizon. You are honour bound to accept my challenge."

Setsek stands with his head held high, back straight. Confidence brimming from every pore. Behind him the fight in the spiral corridors has stopped. He casts a quick glance towards his supporters. None of them have suffered a single blow. Neither have they killed those they were fighting. He nods proudly at them and turns back to Peksur. The challenge has been invoked. No other actions are relevant.

Peksur on the other hand stands still, letting his rage build. Breathing loudly, he clenches his teeth. Setsek's confidence aggravating him further. When he finally speaks, its forced and filled with anger.

"Setsek, I should have known you would not pass by this opportunity. You have been impatiently waiting for this day for years."

Setsek smirks, pleased by the crack he has put in Peksur's composure.

Peksur enraged further by Setesek's callous attitude, takes the lower road.

"I assume you prepared yourself by admiring you reflection in those stones you spend day and night polishing in your room."

Setsek caught unawares by this statement, looks side to side at the commoners and warriors alike. A faint murmur spreads through those present. Peksur just made him look soft in front of the entire Valdasin population. He embarrassed him. But he swallows his anger. He has worked hard for this moment. Trained himself to the point of death. He will not let petty taunts ruin it for him. He responds to Peksur, louder this time, with just a hint of smugness, "Do not stall the inevitable with your pettiness, Peksur. Your hidden Slinger friends cannot help you oppress us any longer. I have seen to it. You must accept the challenge."

> Oh no! The Talons.

Peksur falters for a moment but quickly regains his composure. He takes a deep breath. He sees a way out. With a smile on his face, he shouts for all present to hear, "I surrender."

A wave of shock passes over all present.

> It's rare but not unheard of. Valdasin are a weird group of people. They get all worked up about their honour and traditions, but when convenient, or rather inconvenient, whoosh! Here comes another rule for the tradition. Kind of like the Thread rules forcing me to go through these common fights for power. In the bigger picture, they are rarely consequential.

Setsek is the first to speak, frantic and angry, "No. No, you must fight me. You are not a coward Peksur. You are the Supreme Commander. Do not sully the title. Grow a spine you fool and fight me!"

Peksur calmly replies, unfazed by the raw anger in Setsek's voice, "No Setsek. I have the right to surrender. Perhaps one such as you, with your luxuries, is unaware of the rules for the sacred Trial. Should I explain?"

Peksur is confident now. He stares down Setsek with a wide smile on his face.

"It is the final step of the Trial. The loser, which is me, will be allowed to inflict a non-fatal wound to you," Peksur musters all the contempt he could and pours it into his next words, "the *winner*."

A flicker of fear passes over Setsek's face. He realises the ill intent behind Peksur's surrender.

He pushes aside his fear and straightens himself, taking a step towards Peksur, sword raised.

Peksur, readies himself and speaks aloud, fear lacing his words, "Setsek, I Supreme Commander Peksur, surrender to you in front of our people. As is my right under the Trial of Two Edges, I demand the right of the last..."

No! Coward!

Before Peksur could complete his words, Setsek steps forward and rams his sword upwards through his ribs. A look of pure hatred flickers across Peksur's face before it slumps lifeless towards Setsek.

The Valdasin gathered look on in stunned silence. No one dares make a sound at this blatant disregard of their most sacred rites. The entire gathering, even the soldiers who, moments ago, were fighting for Peksur. No one cares.

> The apathy, the blatant disregard for duty and loyalty. Its unfathomable.

Setsek slowly pulls out his sword and lets Peksur fall to the ground unceremoniously. He turns to the crowd gathered at the walls.

"The old traditions die today. Peksur, the last Supreme Commander of the noble bloodline tainted by magic is dead. Today we take back Valdas from all that would harm us. Today marks the beginning of a new chapter for all of Valdas. Death to the Talons. Death to the Slingers."

The cry is taken up by all present.

> For all their talk of honour, Valdasin have none. They might have traded one tyrant for another by their continuing apathy. And it does not bode well for the Talons.
>
> Does our friend Rakh have an inkling of what has transpired in his own backyard? Let us find out.

Chapter 19

Thread: Rakh

Location: Svarka

> No way! I missed out on all the fun stuff. They are just sitting and talking again.

Sunten and Rakh are seated at a table opposite each other. Rubio has pulled his chair off to the side. Blocking the path to the exit. Agni and Dvija have cleaned up and seated in the kitchen section of the hideaway.

> I say section because apparently, Rubio is not a big fan of walls. Maybe he took the saying that walls have ears to heart.

The entire hideaway is segregated into neat and exact sections using lines on the ground. A section to cook, a section to sleep. A section to have serious discussions with friends and crooks alike. A door that, thankfully, goes to the one section separated by walls. And the exception to the rule. There are no other inner walls. Not even a flimsy one. It's all just there, all together in a single big hall.

The children are evidently quite famished. From the looks pile of used dishes by them, they have already devoured enough food to last them a week.

> They should be careful though. Too much food after being famished can be just as bad as being hungry. It can be painful. I speak from personal experience of course. Recent personal experience.

Rubio and Rakh are staring at Sunten. Rubio in particular is adamant at not moving his gaze from Sunten, despite subtle signals from Rakh to let them speak in whatever privacy a wall-less meeting room can provide. Sunten is all jittery. Flicking his eyes from Rakh to Agni and Dvija. But for reasons unknown, he does not dare turn to look at Rubio.

"Look, I am telling you, just let them go. They know nothing. They are just children," Sunten breaks the silence.

Rakh spares a glance at the children before continuing his unnerving stare at Sunten.

"You know, you are not what I expected," Rakh says leaning back in his chair, "not at all. Too much compassion for a Nirdak."

Rakh flinches ever so slightly as Sunten slams the table with both his hands. Behind Sunten, Rubio is on his feet in an instant and takes a stride towards Sunten. Rakh signals both of them to calm down. Rubio stops but continues to stand — closer to Sunten than before.

Sunten stares at Rakh for a few more moments before raising both his hands in peace and slumps back in his chair. Only then does Rubio let down his guard and move back to his seat behind Sunten.

"One more outburst like that and I snap you like a twig!" Rubio mutters from behind.

Sunten jumps up in his seat, alert. But still in a foul mood, he speaks up, "I know it's hard for you to believe, but I am not..." A cough from Rubio interrupts him. He sighs and nods his head.

"...I am no longer," he pauses, having difficulty even saying the next words aloud.

"A Nirdak," he says in a very faint whisper.

"I find that hard to believe," Rakh says after a brief pause.

"Nirdak are not the sort to let someone simply leave their cult. Its unheard of."

Sunten lets out a slight grunt," You are right there. They would never let anyone leave."

Rubio lets out a loud "Aha!"

A slight rebuke from Rakh silences him again. Sunten patiently waits for Rubio to settle down before he continues, “Sure, there have been instances of an individual or two, escaping the Nirdak holds, But, escaping their company. It is — not enough. The rituals that each Nirdak goes through are unbreakable. And the likes which will almost instantly expose a Nirdak.”

Sunten pauses. Waiting for Rubio to react again.

“So, you are still a Nirdak?” Rakh taunts Sunten. Trying to keep him off balance in the conversation.

Sunten to his credit, does not rise to the jibe. He unconsciously moves his hand to his eye patch before catching himself. He calmly continues, " I found a way to break the hold of the ritual. I am still bonded by its words, but they can no longer force me to do anything. They are benign, like a venom less snake or a toothless hound!”

With the last statement, Sunten seems to relax a bit. He sits up straight in his chair. Matching Rakh’s stare with confidence.

Behind Sunten, Rubio was keenly listening to Sunten. Waiting for Sunten to elaborate further. A few moments in, he starts visibly shaking. He stares a hole through Sunten’s back.

"Well tell us how you did it boy." Rubio yells. Agni and Dvija who were outside the conversation till now, jump in their chairs. Sunten twists in his chair to look at Rubio with wide eyed shock. Rakh unmoved, simply nods towards the children.

Rubio turns to see the children looking at him in shock as well. He had been nothing but pleasant to them till now. He replaces his frown with a toothy smile and settles back in his chair. He indicates Rakh to continue his questioning.

Rakh still leaning back in his chair. Calm and in control looks at Sunten. "What my excitable friend here —" Rubio rolls his eyes at Rakh "wants to know, is that how did you manage to mitigate the ritual's effect."

Rubio leans forward, waiting for Sunten to answer. However, Sunten leans back in to his chair. and refuses to acknowledge Rubio, instead looking pointedly at Rakh.

"No," he says and continues to sit in silence.

Behind him, Rubio is taken aback. He was not expecting this kind of response from Sunten. Rakh on the opposite side looks amused by the whole situation. He gestures to Rubio to stay calm, never shifting his gaze from Sunten.

When no further response is forthcoming from Sunten, Rakh speaks up, "I like this confidence you have mustered in the last few minutes, but I wouldn't test Rubio's patience too much. You have just hinted at a very important piece of information."

Rakh leans forward. He tells Sunten to come forward as well and lowers his voice to a whisper. "There is a long trail of injuries and broken bones left by Rubio in his search for the information you have conveniently confirmed you possess."

Sunten is taken aback by Rakh's words. He turns to look at Rubio who is once again staring at him, arms crossed, nostrils flared. He looks to Rakh, then to Agni and Dvija who have yet to notice this part of the conversation. His eyes go wide as he realises something. A smirk forms on Sunten's face. He raises his head and meets Rakh's stern gaze. Defiant, he speaks up, "You almost had me there. But you need better lies. His reputation —" Still starting at Rakh, he flicks his thumb towards Rubio, "— his *real* reputation precedes him."

Rakh raises an eyebrow at Sunten, not letting his expressions soften, "His real reputation?"

Undaunted, Sunten forges ahead. He speaks in a mocking tone, "Yes, his real reputation. He makes a show of being ruthless, but he would never harm me as long as the children are here. He wouldn't hurt his food if he could help it."

> I don't know where he got his information from but it's missing a lot of detail. If he could see the Delves, I have seen, he would think twice before playing this game with either of these two.

Rubio looks at him in disbelief. Rakh is stifling a laugh.

Sunten still on his confident roll, continues, "Besides, I would have to be a fool. Why would I give up the greatest secret in all of Sukarsha to the two of you? In the last few hours, you," he says pointing at Rakh," have chased me down like a pack of wolves on a hunt of a lifetime and this guy," now pointing at Rubio," won't even give me a drink of water, and all the while boring holes in the back of my head with his stares."

Seeing them looking at him in silence, Sunten pushes his luck further, "The information has great meaning to you. If you want it, I want something in return. No not something! A lot of things. Whatever I ask for."

Rakh amused by Sunten's attitude, mocks him,

"Do tell in the name of the three gods, what can we offer you for this very important information? It seems you have my friend in a stranglehold. I have never seen him so dumbfounded since the day of his marriage!"

Without picking up the subtle tones of sarcasm in Rakh's voice, Sunten chances a glance at Rubio. He sees Rubio giving him an open-mouthed stare. Satisfied with the effect he has had on Rubio; he smiles to himself and turns to face Rakh with confidence.

"It is clear that you are the brains behind this little operation. Too bad you went against me. But I am not as rude as your friend there. I will let you win some too. I believe in fairness. I will give you the information you want. I warn you though. It's not for the weak-hearted. I could not go through with it for five months," he says, holding out his hand with his fingers spread in front of Rakh's face.

"But I stood firm in my resolve. And finally, I made it. Take the information and do with it as you please. But don't blame me if whomever you want out of the Nirdak, doesn't have the resolve to follow through. There's no going back either way once you step on this path," he finishes.

Mistakenly believing that he has bested Rakh, he confidently leans over to take Rakh's untouched mug of water and takes a deep gulp out of it. Then, in a not-so-subtle game of chicken, Sunten waits for Rakh or Rubio to speak. Rubio breaks first, unable to contain his impatience," Fine! Fine! you got us. Now tell us what you want in return for this information."

Sunten gives a sly smile to Rakh and says," Not much. Just give me all the money you have in your hideaway here. You can keep the smaller coins. I do have an idea of what you have hidden away here...Hoarder," he says the last word with condemnation. As if suggesting that Rubio was just as bad as a Nirdak for being a part of the Murder.

He continues," The children leave with me. Once we are out of Svarka, I will find the nearest messenger and send you the information you seek. These are my terms. Accept them or do whatever you want with us. You are not getting the information you seek any other way."

On the other side of the *room* Agni and Dvija have finally had their fill. For the past short while, they have been attentively listening to Sunten talking down to Rakh and Rubio. From time to time, they giggle. Finding the situation funny. However, when they hear him talk about leaving, they share a panicked look. After being hungry for days on end, they did not want to leave the one place where they could get their fill.

They rush towards Rubio and speak up in unison," No Sunten. We don't want to leave Rubio. You stay here too. He promised us he wouldn't hurt you. And...and... that they would only pretend to scold you, so you don't do anything bad anymore."

They look up at Rubio and plead to him "Didn't you say that Rubio? Tell him. Tell him now or he will take us from here. We don't want to leave!"

Rubio looks at the children in shock. He is once again at a loss of words. He looks at Rakh who is now thoroughly enjoying himself. Then back at the children and then back at Rakh. Finally, he gives a big shrug and slumps down. He smiles at the children and pats their heads.

Sunten is looking around the room in bewilderment. He makes wild pointing actions at the children and Rubio and then at Rakh.

Sunten's wild actions are interrupted by the sounds of a bellow of laughter. All eyes turn towards Rakh, who is laughing uncontrollably. As he catches everyone's stare on him, he sits up and says, "This is only the second time one of my plans has been foiled. And same as last time, this one was also foiled by children." He breaks into another bout of laughter.

> Oh, he is lying. He has definitely had more than two foiled plans. I know. I have Delved his past quite thoroughly. And this is the first time it has been because of children. Typical adult behaviour, when in doubt blame a child. Rubbish.

Sunten sinks into his chair. All his earlier confidence has evaporated.

"You two, you two want to stay here?"

Sunten asks incredulously. He shakes his head in disbelief, then a thought occurs to him. With a hint of anger, he questions them again, "Did these two animals threaten you with something to make you say this? Don't worry at all. They can't do anything to you as long as I am here. They wouldn't dare."

Agni and Dvija shake their head in response.

Sunten speaks up again, "I... I don't know what to say." He looks at Rakh and Rubio in turn and speaks in an accusatory tone," You two — you two have done something to them. What have you done? How could you?"

"Nothing. Now sit down while I explain the predicament you find yourself in."

> See I told you we missed the exciting part. This part's all talk! Talk! Dhat! I am tired of writing all this blabber. Let's just let them talk to each other while I rest my hand. Doesn't look like these three could do anything interesting for now if they tried.

Chapter 20

Before we get back to the comedy trio of Rakh, Rubio and Sunten and their support cast Agni and Dvija, I want to answer a question I know has been gnawing away at you since you started reading this book.

How is this young and talented child surviving by himself in what is essentially in the middle of nowhere surviving?

It has to be worrying you to no end, right?

Otherwise, what kind of a foul and heartless person would you have to be to read a book written by a child who continuously mentions his appalling situation and not care for their well-being?

I believe I have said enough that by now you should have welled up with sympathy and concern for my health. Any normal person would need far less reason than what I have already given.

So let me put your bleeding heart to rest. You should not worry. I am fairly well-fed and completely safe. Indulge me while I tell you a little about our home, Satraksh.

You should keep notes by the way. Make a nice notebook for summarising everything. I know I am not.

Anyway, Satraksh. It's close to where this volume of the Chronicle began. Anthala. Don't ask me if this location was chosen for being close to a font of power or if the font exists because of Satraksh. I do not have an inkling about our history. Aside from what I learnt through my fascination for the unexplained and anomalous volumes of the Chronicle to really pay attention to *our* history.

So, near the outer edge of the cave system, wherever the chamber roof was low and relatively thinner, the Krihaani engineers had built a shaft outwards through the roof. These shafts would allow natural light to come through, and mechanisms were placed to allow air flow throughout Satraksh. At the base of these numerous shafts, were placed patches of arable soil. Allowing us to grow what we could. These would be mostly hardy plants that needed little water or sunlight. But these would not be enough. Not for the thousand strong population that resided here.

And to allay that concern, I present to you our stores. Throughout the vast system of caverns, smaller chambers were constructed into the walls to hold resources we could not grow or scavenge from the grove at our doorstep. Replenished by a supply run made by the elders once every month. And lucky for me, the biggest stores are right here in the main cavern.

In the darkness, leaving the Chronicle open to function as a beacon, I groped around in the darkness to access the stores. I frequented this area in my function as an apprentice Chronicler. So, I was fairly familiar with the layout. Yet — I did stumble onto — you know. But if I am to perform my duty I must survive. So, pushing aside my guilt and sense of horror, I persevered to reach the stores and carried as much as I could to where I sit to write in the Chronicle.

And ironic as it may seem, lucky for me, the marauders were only interested in killing, the stores are still intact. In fact, they had just been replenished a day — earlier!

A DAY EARLIER!

I am a fool. How could I not have realised this sooner? No. Yes. No. Nooo. Yes. Yes, this is it. The replenishing of our stores. The weak link in our security.

But how?

For thousands of years, the elders have safely brought in outside material. There has never been a lapse before let alone an entire attacking force breaching out defence.

I must find out more details about this. We Krihaani wrote down everything. There must be something written about this replenishment process. Somewhere in the older volumes. Maybe one of our writings will finally be useful.

Once I know what weakness those murdering maniacs exploited, I will be a step closer to finding out who they were and why my parents and my people had to die.

I thank you profusely.

Enjoy this moment of gratitude. Because once the larger mystery of the attackers is solved. You are next in line.

Yes, I will find out more on this soon. I will. But as always, duty comes first. And we must follow the Threads that lead us to the end of the world!

Let's see what our heroic heroes are up to now.

Chapter 21

Thread: Rakh

Location: Outskirts of Svarka

> Just in time! Zirsa is here. Her domineering attitude over Rakh has become a highlight of these Threads for me.

Zirsa's apparition is mid-sentence as I Connect," ...man named Setsek. Our Talon narrowly escaped the men he sent to eliminate them. Peksur was a reluctant ally. But an ally all the same."

> Thank goodness the Talons in Valdas escaped their fate. I still do not trust the Talons as a whole. But no one should have to face their untimely end, simply because of their affiliations.

Rakh is standing on top of a small hill overlooking Svarka. Far outside its boundary. There is no vegetation to speak of for several miles. No large rocks or formations that could keep one out of Rakh's line of sight.

I suppose in a place filled with crooks and opportunists, safe places to have sensitive discussions are hard to come by. Especially if you don't want your allies to listen in either.

Rakh lets out a deep sigh before speaking. "That complicates matters. I was hoping for safe passage through their territories."

Zirsa solemnly nods her head in agreement. "Ideally, I would prefer you stay holed up in Svarka, till Suthrin and Donas could arrive as reinforcements."

Rakh shakes his head, "The Nirdak could make an attempt to capture the Focus at any moment. It is not safe in Svarka. Even the Murder will be hunting for Talons in their midst soon."

"I see," Zirsa says thoughtfully. "Have you confirmed that the Artefact does not react to your Focus? How about the new Focus? No cross-effects with them either I hope?"

Rakh simply nods to affirm her assumptions.

Seems like all the events of late have mellowed both Rakh's and Zirsa's personality. They are not biting off each other's heads like before.

I am bored.

"Then its decided," Zirsa says and starts barking orders to Rakh.

There she is. Almost as if she was royalty.

"Use your Focus to leave Svarka without delay. The Torika Null is your safest option at present. It should not take you more than a day to get here."

As she speaks her image is looking downwards to an unseen map.

Her image looks up at Rakh.

"I will direct Suthrin and Donas to meet and escort you through the Torika..." She breaks off mid-sentence. Rakh is fidgeting in place. A subtle shake of his head catches her eye.

"Out with it Rakh. You are not telling me something."

"It's —" Rakh hesitates.

"It's the two Focus Zirsa. They are not objects. But two living breathing children," he blurts out in a single breath.

Zirsa has no immediate response. She stares at Rakh, slack jawed. She is speechless.

> As she should be. It is common knowledge that the power of a Focus cannot reside in anything living. Similar to the common knowledge that Satraksh was impenetrable. Oh, and that the Paurnik Focus had all been lost.
>
> All <u>very</u> common knowledge.

With no quips forthcoming, Rakh gives a wry smile and says," This is the part where you ask questions Zirsa."

Zirsa takes a deep breath. Not one to let her shock get the better of her, she speaks in a steady but questioning voice, "You are certain?"

Without waiting for a response she continues, "Of course you are. I would not expect you to be mistaken about this."

Rakh nods with a tired smile on his face and replies, "Think hard and you will realise the true implications of their awakening."

For the second time in a single conversation, Zirsa cannot hide her astonishment

"Why children? Not children!"

"It is what it is. But Zirsa — this is a dangerous secret — the first two Focus to be discovered in over five hundred years are children. This cannot get out."

Zirsa nods her agreement. "It will be difficult keeping this under wraps. The council will need to be convinced, but I believe Kintra can help there."

"No. Not Kintra. Not the council. No one!" Rakh says with a force behind his words.

"But, Rakh my oaths..."

He cuts her off, anger creeping into his voice, "Do not think of pushing me on this Zirsa."

He raises his hands to emphasise his every word, "You will not tell anyone about them."

> This is actually serious. I have missed something important. Not seen Rakh lose his composure till now. Get angry, yes, but never lose control of his emotions like this.

A phantom of incredulity leaks through Zirsa's composed façade. But she quickly suppresses it. "Very well. Whatever the cost to me. I will keep the secret. I trusted you to save my life once. I will trust you in this too."

As Zirsa mentions Rakh having saved her life, he immediately calms down. The crack in his composure, gone in the blink of an eye.

"It was once Zirsa. You were a child. I do not hold it over you."

"Once was enough for a lifetime of trust." Zirsa replies, respectfully.

A few moments of silence pass through them, before Zirsa speaks up, a smile on her face, "So I assume you have also decided the path forward? Where should I ask Donas and Suthrin to meet you?"

Rakh grins at Zirsa. "Rubio has arranged passage with a trustworthy trade caravan." Sensing the scepticism on

Zirsa's face, he quickly adds," well as trustworthy as you can get for ones dealing with stolen goods. "

Zirsa, not wanting to push the absurdity of the situation any further, waves of the explanation.

"Do continue with your well thought plan Rakh"

Ignoring the not so subtle jibe, Rakh summarises the next steps, "We will travel with them for a day. On the first night, we will break out of the caravan and cut through the jungle towards the Torika gap in the Null. During this season the trail should be unused. We should be able to reach the gap by the next morning. From the edge of the Null," he pauses, doing rough calculations in his mind, "we will be at the Grove in two days' time."

Despite her obvious qualms about the plan, Zirsa has been making notes on a map in her chambers. Her image hunched over the invisible map, she looks it over once more as Rakh finishes. Moments later she straightens towards Rakh.

"That brings you to the Grove in about four days' time. I would have preferred you keep to the roads. Even if takes a day or two more. The trails will bring you close to one of the Nirdak holds. Are these risks necessary? Sensible?"

> Does she not know who she is speaking to? When has this man ever done anything sensible? Insensible should be his middle name!

Rakh pauses for a moment before replying," Sunten assures me that the Nirdak in that hold are mostly lower-rung members who wouldn't dare leave the hold. I trust him on this."

He pauses to consider Zirsa's observation once more. "Road travel will be faster, sure, but with the upheaval in Valdas, I would not risk running into one of their patrols."

And with a tone of finality that forbade any further discussion, "No, Its final. We go for the Torika gap."

Zirsa nods in acknowledgement, "Very well then. Suthrin and Donas will meet you at the Null border to aide you through it I will expect a daily update from you until you join with them."

Rakh shakes his head at the last statement

"We do not know what kind of detection the Nirdak and the Triumvirate might have deployed near Svarka. Moreover, the two children — untrained as they are — are emanating a persistent aura. Once we leave Svarka, I will have no choice but to suppress everything. I am unsure about its efficacy, but it's the best tool I have at hand to reduce our odds of being discovered."

By now, Zirsa has given up any semblance of having control of the situation. "I am showing a great deal of faith in you Rakh in allowing this plan. Be careful. and good luck. "

Without another word, or waiting for Rakh's response, Zirsa's image disappears and Rakh is left alone staring at thin air. He smiles to himself and disappears in a flash to reappear on a building in Svarka. In contrast to any other town, no thieves or thugs roamed the streets of Svarka at night. Everyone slept peacefully even without proper law enforcement.

Tonight, however, a strange thief roams the streets. Rakh flashes in and out of various shops and warehouses. Picking up items he needs for the journey ahead. What will surprise the owners in the morning will not be the missing items, but what is left behind: exact coin, stacked neatly on their counters.

Chapter 22

Not to lick an empty plate clean, but the logistics of a single Chronicler are maybe, possibly, perchance catching up to us. And by us, I mean me.

I missed canonising something important in the Chronicle.

This when I don't have no other task at present besides writing the Chronicles.

Well maybe one more task. Definitely two more.

However, I am happy to announce that I have made headway on one of them. So let us call this a balanced outcome. Not to mention that missing things, seems to have become a part of the Krihaani legacy now. And I for one will not mess with our legacy.

But — I am getting ahead of myself. Let's step back a bit. I left Rakh's Thread three hours past midnight. So, I figured while he and his soon to be companions rest, I should dedicate these hours towards important research.

As such let us reflect on our last conversation where we stumbled upon a possible chink in the armour that protected Krihaani from the outside world.

Our monthly supply runs from the outside world.

To find out more I decided to make way to our archives. At the core of our polis lies the Tower of Truth.

I do want to mention that I learnt from my last couple of forays into the darkness and improvised. I took the Chronicle with me this time. While I did spend considerable time inside the archives, the path there is not as clear in my mind. The meagre light provided by the Chronicle's glow was enough for me to see the way forward. While keeping the more gruesome visions at the edge of darkness. Where they belong. Something that lighting a torch would not accomplish.

Not to mention, I would definitely need the light to reach the Tower's entrance itself. While the other caverns, occupied by the Krihaani, were regularly cleaned to keep the floor and ceilings free of stalactites and stalagmites, the Tower's cavern was left untouched. It was connected to the rest of the cave system in five directions via small tunnels. Enough for two, maybe three persons to pass shoulder to shoulder. From each tunnel's mouth to the Tower's entrance, the path meandered through a dense arrangement of stalagmites. We were forbidden to touch them.

I reached the Tower via the southern tunnel. Even in the darkness I reflexively looked up towards the Tower's top. Where previously, the Soul of Truth resided. Glowing red, inside a lattice of an unknown alloy. From which multiple wires extruded to branch off across Satraksh. It was a gem of immense power. Powering everything in the entire cave system. From lights, to providing heat. When the caves of Satraksh plunged into darkness during the attack, I immediately knew that the gem was stolen. Was that their sole goal?

Maybe. Maybe not.

Pushing the Soul out of my mind, I moved forward under the Chronicle's glow. Carefully avoiding the stalagmites on the path.

The Tower's doors opened against my weight with a loud creak. Echoing through the cavern and across the connecting tunnels. I was scared stiff at the sound. Hurriedly, I closed my Chronicle. Lest its glow attract attention. After a long time waiting with bated breath, the complete silence that pervades these caves now, gave me the confidence to open the Chronicle once more, and step in.

Normally, the sight of the tower, its grand scale. Something that never ceased to mesmerise me, evoked no feelings today. I could not see the shelves towering over me. I could not see them spiralling away beneath me into the depths of Prathak. I could not see anything in the pitch-black darkness. I could not feel the excitement I always felt.

The tower while only four floors above ground, extended for multiple floors deep underground. And wide. It contains miles of shelves built underneath a major part of Satraksh. Containing everything the Krihaani have written since their inception. Volumes of the Chronicle showcased in all their glory.

Not just that. Even volumes from before the Chronicle itself was created. Writings from the day the aura that protects us, rather the aura that *protected* us was erected. Before Sukarsha was raised. Before the fateful battle of Sriki.

Where, once, each visit would begin with me taking in the grandeur of the Tower and the archives, today, I had but one trivial thing in my mind. Finding information about our supply runs. Supply runs!

But enough detail for now. Seeing as you were resourceful enough to get your hands on this volume of the Chronicle, should your interest rise, go ahead and get those other volumes yourself.

Given my previous experience, I quickly found the volume I needed. The one that contained the entire process of the supply run. And within its pages I found one crucial — staggering fact — that brings me to one inevitable conclusion. The aura's mind wiping was not as exhaustive as we were led to believe.

The Grand Chronicler, if he so desired, could embed an instruction in the mind of a person.

One singular instruction. That would survive all mind wiping effects of the aura once.

They would forget everything else, but that instruction — it would be embedded deep in their mind, leaving them no choice but to follow it through to the end.

If you think about it, logically, it makes sense. How else would someone leaving Satraksh remember for example, to return with supplies for us? If they forgot everything, they would forget us as well as our needs.

So, the need for this singular override, undisputed. But why was this not known to the Krihaani at large? Why, or rather when, did it disappear from our common knowledge? What else has met the same fate?

But I digress.

The instruction.

Makes sense.

Except it doesn't really explain the attackers.

The attackers came from outside the aura. And the volume was clear—the instruction can only be embedded by the Grand Chronicler. Even if he'd wanted to, he couldn't have left Satraksh to embed the instruction. He would've forgotten it.

So how?

Am I missing something?

Is this even the crack in the aura that they used to execute my people?

The more I unravel these threads, the more tangled they become. Will I ever realise the complete truth of my people's fate? Or as a Krihaani, I am destined to only observe the fates of others?

Only time will tell. What little of it is left to me.

And within that time, I must see to my duty. As much as I wish to rest after this short but tiring trip through Satraksh, I must keep moving. I need to record first-hand what transpired between Rakh and Sunten. Lest I be unfortunate enough — maybe fortunate in some ways — to have a young upstart judge my Chronicle as I judged Chronicler Paurak.

And to that end, we are going to perform a Delve.

Chapter 23

Thread: Rakh (Delve)

Location: Svarka

You are in luck. Usually, when a Chronicler wanted a Delve, they would ask one of their subordinates to do it for them and have them file the record into a separate Delve registry. The subordinate would then inform the Chronicler about the Delve's identifier in the registry. This entire process was mostly for posterity. Rarely would a Chronicler review the registry for a Delve they requested.

A common belief held by my predecessors was that anything not presented through the Connections could not be worth recording.

The result?

The truth, hidden. Omitted. Unseen.

Not the legacy I wanted for my people.

Neither will I tarnish it by my hand.

So, for the first time, in my knowledge, a Delve is being recorded directly into the Chronicle.

Oh, if my father saw me now. He was a stickler for processes and protocols. But he can't. Not anymore. I can do what I want and record the Delve right here. And you my trusted friend will be the first person to read it. Be proud.

Well, enough of my sob story, even if it is littered with knowledge previously reserved for the Krihaani alone.

Let's Delve.

I chose Rakh, because from what I recall, his position would have had the widest view of the hideaway.

I have gone back almost to the instant I had broken the Connection with Rakh.

Agni and Dvija join the three adults. They have just as much at stake as anyone else, more so, since they are the ones, the discussion is about. Agni stands next to Rubio. Dvija has pulled his chair to sit beside him. Rakh and Sunten at the table. Sunten is in a sullen mood. His confidence high has crashed. He sits cross armed, staring at the mug in front of him.

As a Chronicler in training, I had been tasked with multiple Delves. The sensory limitations within a Delve are different for each person. But never have I seen one as detailed as this.

Almost as if I am performing a Connection instead.

Rakh snaps his fingers at Sunten to get his attention on him. He is all business like. Cold, calm and level.

"You seem to have stumbled upon the first two Focus to have awakened in the last five hundred years," Rakh began, "And somehow involved two innocent children in this dangerous mess."

He casts a glance towards Agni and Dvija. They are looking at Sunten. Anxious and fidgeting. There is concern in their eyes. Agni looks to Rubio, who gives her a reassuring smile.

"The only reason you are not bound and gagged in a corner is because Agni and Dvija seem to think you are a good person. And I always trust the instinct of children."

Sunten shifts in place. Not saying a word. Not meeting Rakh's gaze...

"For instance, children love me. Adore me even. Never met a child who didn't like me," Rakh says as a matter of fact.

Behind Sunten Rubio lets out a snort and both Agni and Dvija squeak out a giggle. Rakh glares at Rubio. Beside him, Dvija looks away and focuses on his feet with great intensity. Rubio pats his head and says, "Don't worry Dvija. He is all show."

Rakh shakes his head, mildly annoyed.

"If you could prevent further interruptions, I would like to get this situation sorted before the Nirdak come knocking at your doors."

Upon mention of the Nirdak, Sunten winces and even Agni who had so far seemed to be in control, shies away behind Rubio and starts looking here and there as if expecting one to appear right in front of her.

"Will you quit dropping that name so frequently," Sunten yells as he stands to tower over Rakh. Not intimidated by this sudden outburst, Rakh meets his stare. Unable to lock eyes with Rakh for long, Sunten blinks and sits back. He clenches and unclenches his fists continuously while taking deep breaths to calm himself down.

"Fine!" he says with frustration, "Fine, I will tell you everything you want to know."

He casts a sideways glance at the children, his frustration quickly replaced by concern, "But you have to give me an oath. Whatever happens, you will keep the children safe."

Rakh looks at Sunten for a moment, without saying anything. Then he nods in agreement.

"Yes. you have my Oath. Even if it costs me my life, I will see to it that these children are seen safely to the Grove. I know of no other place that would be safer for them."

Sunten thinks for a moment.

"And you will give me refuge in Vaasat. No questions asked."

"I hardly believe that you are in a position to keep making demands of me," Rakh says with a subtle harshness.

"But, neither will these children allow me to leave you behind. So be it," he says with a wave of his hand.

Pleased with himself, Sunten sits up straight. He takes a gulp from the mug in front of him and lets out a contented sigh. He puts the mug down with some force.

> He is not very smart, is he? We came here the long way round, but for him it's been a short while. When Rakh put him in place. And here he is. Once more thinking he has gotten the better of him?
>
> I am literally shaking my head right now in disbelief.

Rakh lets out an impatient grunt.

Not wanting to annoy Rakh further, Sunten starts talking.

"Very well. Let's start with the bigger of your misinformed opinions. There are no Focus here. At least not in the way you think of them."

Rakh looks to Agni and Dvija and back to Sunten. Seeing the confusion on his face, Sunten gives a smug smile and says, "You see, Agni and Dvija themselves are the Focus."

As Rakh opens his mouth to ask a question, Sunten raises a hand to stop him.

"Don't ask me how. I only know that it is so."

Sunten looks at Agni and Dvija before quickly turning back to face Rakh. There is a guilt in his eyes every time he looks at them.

"Few years ago. Not too far north of Svarka. We were sent there to raze the village. Instructed to leave nothing standing. No survivors."

Sunten stares into the distance, as if the images of the day were playing in front of him.

"All but four of us entered the village. Looting and pillaging. I could not bring myself to enter. I did not have the stomach. Then our leader — I don't know his name. I was just an initiate at the time — he ordered the entire village to be set on fire."

Sunten's eyes widen as he recollects the memories from the incident. His breathing shallow.

"It was gruesome. Cruel. We were ordered to bar the doors from outside. The villagers — they had fortified their village. Large gates. Large walls made with sharpened timber. Many tried to escape, only to be —"

He snaps his eyes shut and lowers his head. His voice hoarse with emotion, "The fools. They had created a trap for themselves. They could not escape the fire. All of them, burnt alive in their own homes."

He pauses for a moment to get a hold of himself. "I was near the gates. Left alone by the others. They had spread around the village walls to find and hunt any would be escapees."

"That was when I head a scratching noise coming from the side of the gate," Sunten says, pointing in the air, with his right hand. His eyes still unfocused. Still replaying the images of that dreadful day.

"There was a door there. A smaller door. To allow individuals to pass through without opening the larger ones. I looked around to make sure no one else was around. I quickly unbarred it, hoping to let someone — anyone escape."

Agni steps forward to take Sunten's hand in hers. "It was me and Dvija."

"What?" Rakh exclaims.

Agni nods. Still by Sunten's side. He smiles thankfully at her and continues.

"Yes. I can only call it a miracle. They had managed to reach the gate unscathed by the fire. Even a couple steps behind them, lay the charred body of a woman. But they were unharmed."

With tears welling up in his eyes he looked to Agni and Dvija in turn.

"I took them and at great risk escaped to Svarka. And here we stayed — leading an uneventful life — till now." With this he takes a deep sigh. He hands his head with his eyes closed. He has said all he will on the matter for now.

> This all is certainly related to the void Thread. Does It mean that that entire Thread is born of this single incident? But what of the snake headed monster? How does that play in? And what of Rakh's influence on the Thread? Why did it flare only when Rakh was unconscious?
>
> I will need answers to these questions as well.
>
> There is more to this tale. I can sense it. But no one seems to be willing to ask the difficult questions. At least not in front of the children.

Rubio breaks the uncomfortable silence.

"Almost checks out. I know you have been here for almost three years. But it leaves a lot unanswered. One, how you left behind the Ni.." He catches himself, casts a concerned glance at Dvija before continuing,

"How you left behind *their* bindings and how these two came to possess the power of two strong Focus?"

"I will give you the answer to the first in all its gory detail. But I will only give it to you in writing. And you must promise to never repeat it out loud too."

Sunten pauses until Rubio nods in agreement and then continues, "For the second question, the answer is simple — I don't know."

Rubio lets out a snort of disbelief. Before Rubio could say anything Rakh began, "There must be some more you can tell us. It cannot be a coincidence that *they* attacked that specific village. Even for them, the scale of their action — it's an atypical act of violence."

Agni has moved back to comfort Dvija. He has been feeling uncomfortable with this talk of violence. Dvija recedes into himself, while Agni steadies him with a hand. Sunten just shrugs. Guilt weighing him down.

"I honestly do not know. It was merely a coincidence that I found them in that village."

Rakh is in deep thought, suddenly he jerks his head up and looks towards the kitchen section. Suddenly alert, he looks around trying to find something. Not finding anything out of the ordinary, he looks back to Sunten.

> Strange. It felt like he saw or heard something. But I never did. Even though I should have through the Delve.

"We will figure out the why later. For now, answer the when. When did you find out that they were Focus? Our encounter was not the first time you had seen them use their abilities."

Sunten gives a solemn shake of his head. "No, it wasn't. The first time was a few months ago. And I don't know if these powers came to both at the same time, but Agni displayed her powers first."

He takes a breath and presses on, speaking faster now, eager to pass on the information.

"We were going back to our hovel after a day of... erm, *work* at the market. That was when two of the Court's enforcers started following us. Brandishing weapons."

A deep-rooted fear crosses his face.

"We ducked into the alleys as soon as we could. But in our panic ended up at a dead end."

His voice drops slightly. "The enforcers they took everything, but..."

He paused, swallowing hard.

"But they weren't happy. One of them pushed me aside and went for Dvija."

His hands clenched.

"That's when it happened."

He looks directly at Rakh now, the words tumbling out in a single breath.

"Agni screamed. A high, sharp sound that chilled me to my bones. And with the scream came a gust of wind—fierce, sudden. It slammed both enforcers into the opposite wall."

He exhaled.

"Knocked them out cold."

"We ran like death herself was chasing us. I did not look back."

Sunten sits there silently. Tears well up in Agni's eyes but she quickly wipes them away.

"A few months ago? Do you recall if it had been the night of the Tiridel double eclipse?" Rakh asked Sunten," Think carefully. This could be important."

Sunten shook his head.

"I am sorry, but I am not sure. I have rarely kept track. But it could be towards the end of Tiridel. Few of the farmer traders had started coming in with fresh harvests."

Rakh gives a slight nod and leans back. He gestures to Sunten to continue. But before Sunten could say anything Rakh snaps up, suddenly alert and looks towards the back section of the hideaway. The hideaway like most buildings in this section of Svarka was built into the hills that ran through this side of Svarka. He surveys the entire room but sees nothing but rock.

> I think he is just trying to throw the others off by acting this way. I didn't see or hear anything from that direction. If there was anything he could see or hear, even distractedly, I would sense it too.

"OK, this will do. Rest for a while. All of you," he says looking pointedly at the children, "We leave Svarka in the morning."

Before anyone could object, he explains, "If it's been months since the powers manifested, then we are already too late. They were probably not strong enough for the Eyes to Sense sooner, but Nir...*those people* rely on something far more dangerous."

"Rats," he says with spite, "of the worst kind."

Sunten and the children are visibly confused, but Rubio nods solemnly.

"Despite the illegal nature of your powers, even in Svarka, I don't suppose you have completely refrained from using them? Maybe at a sleight of hand trick or two?"

Sunten and Agni look sheepishly set each other. Sunten nods and says, “Maybe a few quick tricks for the days where I could make nothing through other means.”

Rakh nods and says, “I wouldn’t expect an initiate to be aware. But a few months’ time is enough for one of the Rats to convey news of your presence to them. I would leave immediately if I could,” he looks at Agni and Dvija and sighs.

“But travelling with children will be difficult. I will spend tonight making the necessary arrangements. We leave tomorrow at all costs.”

Rubio looks dejectedly towards Rakh and then towards Sunten. Rakh notices and walks to his friend. In a low tone, he tells him, “I am sorry my friend. I know what Sunten’s information means to you, and I promise, we will accomplish what needs to be done.”

Rakh pauses to put a hand on Rubio’s shoulder, “Speak to him tonight and find out what you need. But acting on it will have to wait. I cannot risk their lives.”

Rubio looks up at Rakh and nods. A glint of sadness in his eyes, which is quickly replaced by a hardened expression, “And I would never ask that of you. I know you are a man of your word Rakh. Once Sunten gives me the information I need, I will begin preparations and call for you once I am ready.”

Sunten listening in on the conversation, speaks up, "Why do you care so much about this? No one cares about us. Despite the fear, most would consider us no better than maggots!"

Rakh looks to Sunten, his tone filled with grief, "I am sure you have heard of Ardeo of the Sorni protectorate?"

A flicker of fear passes over Sunten's face and a pang of guilt over Rubio's.

Sunten nods his head and says, "Yes. Extremely well. A ruthless leader."

Rakh looks Sunten in the eyes and says, "That man is Rubio's brother. And I will do anything to help him get his brother back."

> The heartbreak of losing family is impossible to heal for most. I like Rubio. I hope he can get what he wants.

Sunten looks down, embarrassed about his earlier outburst. "I am sorry, I did not know. I will give you all you need to break him free of his bond."

He takes a deep breath, as if about to say something difficult, "But before anything else, you should know two things."

He raises his finger, speaking with a hard edge, "One, the act needed to make the ritual ineffective is irreversible," He waves of Rubio before he could say anything, "Yes, yes. It sounds like an obvious decision, but it's not."

Rubio gives a nod of acceptance.

"And two, the decision will have to be his. You cannot force the act on him or threaten him into it. It will have to be done of his free will."

He repeats himself, more emphatically this time, "This is important. If he goes through the ritual with even an iota of doubt — the ritual *will* fail — and there will not be another chance."

Rakh looks at both in turn. "You two have much to discuss then. Let the children rest. I will take care of preparations for our departure."

Without another word or before someone else can say anything, Rakh disappears in a flash.

> Bah. I wanted to learn of the ritual for posterity as well. Maybe I should have Delved in to Rubio instead. Too late now. Its only two turns till sunrise. I must rest before Rakh begins his journey towards the Null. If I remember Zirsa's map correctly, there are more ways than one his journey could come to an end.

Chapter 24

It seems I have rested much longer than I intended to. The fatigue of the past few days finally caught up to me. Not to mention the difficulty in keeping track of time inside a dark place. The timekeepers have gone silent too. Powerless without the Soul, like all other devices in Satraksh.

Since that dreaded day — the only way I have had to know the passage of time, has been through the Connections.

The archives as I noticed in my last visit, were by fortune's grace entirely unspoiled by those monsters. Except for the vandalism outside the Tower to obtain the Soul. As far as I could tell, they did not even step inside.

And that is why after thorough consideration, today, I have shifted my base of operations to the archives. I carried the Chronicle and as much of my supplies as I could to the main hall of the Tower of Truth.

The stench of death and decay near the Grand Chronicler's statue had become unbearable. Same with the other caverns I visited. And the silence only amplified the cries of my people that continue to ring through my ears. Taunting me. Reminding me what I have lost.

At the very least being close to these older volumes might give me a semblance of being close to my kin.

Misguided as they were in their efforts to make these records, they are still fruits of their labour. Countless hours spent in the name of duty over thousands upon thousands of years.

I do not think I will outlive the guilt of surviving my people. Somehow, I feel there is one other person we know of, who perhaps shares the emotion, if not the circumstances.

Every mile that they put between themselves and Svarka, causes Sunten's Thread continues to glow brighter.

Why, one might ask.

I have not a clue.

All I can do for now is to decide, whether or not to Connect to his Thread.

Chapter 25

Thread: Sunten

Location: Torika wildlands

It is just past sunset. The caravan has stopped for the day. They have all separated into their own smaller groups. Unorganised. There is no watch. No lookouts. Either they are not afraid of danger or believe themselves to be the most dangerous ones out here.

Sunten is sitting at a small fire next to a wagon with Agni and Dvija. It is close to the edge of the camp. Rakh is nowhere to be seen. Dvija is resting against the wagon's wheel. Exhausted and half asleep. Agni is sitting beside Sunten, idly pulling grass from the ground.

> I suppose it was difficult to notice in Svarka. Given that everything was so densely packed and right in your face. But out here, in the open, its pronounced. Connecting to Sunten, it's a little bit jarring. The depth of objects is not that clear. Things on one side are out of focus. Not because of his link to that strange nightmare — I hope. Rather because of his disability. He only has one eye — did I not mention that earlier? I

wonder why something similar has never been mentioned in any of the earlier volumes I have read.

Strange. And speaking of strange...

The three of them are in the company of a stranger. An elderly man, cooking over the fire. He is hunched over, and frail. But his movements are quick. Alert. As if they are still catching up to his age. His clothes are old. Colours faded, but they still seem to be sturdy. The material having withstood the tests of time.

"Never seen you on this route before," the man says as he stirs the stew. His voice is low and hoarse. But friendly.

Feeling ambushed by the question, Sunten finds himself scrambling for an answer that would not raise suspicion.

"We are traders. We trade in goods from Svarka. We are on our way to Valdas."

The man lets out a low chuckle.

"You like hunting for fish in the jungle too I presume. This route goes to the Sorni protectorate."

Before Sunten could dig himself a deeper hole, the elderly man stops him.

"Your business is yours. I was just looking for conversation while the stew cooked," he says without looking up from the stew. He adds seasoning to the stew and stirs it some more. The aroma catches the attention of Agni. Even Dvija sits up, salivating at the stew.

"It's ready," the man says with a clap of his hand. He looks at Agni and Dvija.

"These two look like they could use some good food. Tell you what, you give me your names, and I will give you three piping hot bowls of the best stew this side of the barrier."

Without waiting for Sunten's confirmation, Agni announces their names.

"I am Agni. That there is Dvija and this is Sunten. Then there is..."

"That's enough Agni," Sunten interrupts her.

> A good thing he did. These three might not be known enough outside their limited circle. But Rakh on the other hand, most definitely has a reputation that spreads far and wide. Beat not to announce his name to every stranger on the road.

The man laughs at her excitement. He starts ladling the stew into three wooden bowls. "My — *teacher* used to say. Never give away anything good for free. Always get something equally good in return."

He hands a bowl to Dvija, the Sunten and finally to Agni. "You have beautiful names."

Sunten narrows his eyes at the man. He sniffs the stew. Even though both children are eager to dig in, they wait for Sunten. Sensing their hesitation, the man quickly ladles himself a bowl of the stew and starts eating. Sunten too follows suit. After taking a couple spoonful, he nods to Agni and Dvija to proceed.

After her first spoon, Agni exclaims," This is delicious. I love it."

The man lets out a hearty laugh. "I knew you would. The secret is in the seasoning."

He picks a rucksack placed by his side and starts rummaging about. Dvija looks on in fascination. Agni is completely focused on enjoying the stew while Sunten is barely holding back his suspicious stare. After a few moments the man lets out a triumphant cry and brings out a large purple flower. Its bigger than the man's hand. Conical in shape. Three golden filaments growing in the middle, surrounded by multiple layers of petals.

"I use this flower to make the seasoning. It has a name lost to time. Commoners like myself call it Mother's Tear. Make it into a powder form and it will make sewage water taste like the finest wine."

Sunten spurts out the stew from his mouth.

The man laughs at Sunten's reaction.

"Don't worry. I only use fresh spring water for my stew."

He turns his attention to Dvija now," This flower itself is also quite useful. Eat these filaments raw, and they will counteract almost any form of poison. Cover a wound with these petals and it will heal in a day."

Agni and Dvija both look at the flower in awe. Even Sunten has a look of wonder in his eyes.

The elderly man has hooked his audience. "It's quite rare you know. Only found in the deepest parts of the jungles of Rishak. And to keep their efficacy, they must be plucked on the day of a double eclipse," he says to reel them in.

Rare indeed. It's one of a mere five plants whose every single appearance in a Chronicle is catalogued separately. I will have to catalogue this appearance the first chance I get.

> This man, his Thread does not show as important. Its lost amongst one of the numerous Threads criss-crossing the pattern near Svarka. But I have a feeling deep down, that he should be part of the record. Hopefully Sunten has his wits about him and finds out details about him that I can use to Delve and find out more.

Agni is the first one to speak," can I hold it?"

The man makes a show of hesitating and thinking about her request, then with a smile he hands it over to Agni.

Agni carefully turns the flower around. Adoring it from every angle. The man waits a moment before giving an offer," tell you what. I will give you this flower. This very rare flower and in return you give me — let's say, a recently harvested spinehead quill. They are just as rare as this flower."

Agni snaps up to look at the man with a large smile. She turns to Sunten. Before Sunten can say anything, she turns to her brother and winks at him," Dvija, get one of those spinehead quills from the wagon and give it to him."

Sunten stares slack jawed at Agni. He shakes his head vigorously. Lowering his voice to a whisper," No Agni. You know what Rakh said."

The elderly man acts nonchalant. Seemingly enjoying his stew. Smiling at Agni.

Agni returns his smile in kind and turns to Sunten. Pleading with him.

"Please Sunten. He will never know. It's just once. And you heard what he said about the flower."

Not one to disappoint them, Sunten finally relents. He nods at Dvija, who rushes to the back of the wagon. And moments later umps out of the wagon while holding a spinehead quill in his hand.

The elderly man asks with incredulity," You had one? Just lying around?"

Dvija nods vigorously and hands over the quill to the man without a word. The man scrutinises the quill from every angle. Finally satisfied, he looks to Agni, "Deal struck. The flower is yours."

The man stands up and makes to leave, when Sunten remarks, "We never got your name sir."

Stopping a step away from the campfire, the man turns back towards Sunten and gives a sad smile. "Indeed, you did not."

He gives it a moment of thought. "Unfortunately, you do not have anything else you could give me for it. Perhaps — the next time we meet."

With this he walks away, without another look towards Sunten and the children.

> And there goes my chance to find information to Delve him. It is truly frustrating. When people do not do exactly what you want them to do. I could Delve into each of the Thread that criss-cross near Sunten at this moment and hope to find the right one. But that is time I do not have.

As Sunten, is deep in thought, reflecting on the strange encounter, he is lifted in the air by his collar from behind. He scrambles to balance himself and turns to come face to face with an enraged Rakh.

"What did you do?" Rakh says with an angry growl. He is taking quick breaths, eyes wide, he is visibly shaking, trying to control himself.

"I gave you one instruction. One."

He turns to Agni and Dvija who are cowering by the wagon. Trembling in fear. He lets Sunten go instantly and steps back. He moves to soothe Agni and Dvija, but they shy away from him and run to Sunten. Rakh lowers his head and looks away in shame.

He takes a moment to calm himself down and turns to Sunten, "I apologise. But you have made a grave mistake. Why did they use the power of the Focus?"

The three do not reply.

"I leave you three to scout the way ahead and you mess things up within moments," Rakh says. Raising his hands in frustration.

"Did you not realise that me stepping away would also take you out of the suppression field's influence? Without using you power you would have been undetected amongst the other hidden Slingers in this caravan. But now. Who knows."

Sunten finally builds up the courage to reply. "I am sorry Rakh. I did not realise. Don't blame them. It's all my fault."

Beside him Agni takes a step forward, defiantly staring down Rakh. "No, it was me. I made Dvija change his hair to spinehead quills so that we could exchange it for the flower."

Rakh looks at the three of them in turn. Eyes wide with astonishment. He opens and closes his mouth to say something but stops himself for a moment.

"A flower? You risked all our lives for a flower?" Rakh says. Anger rising again. He starts shaking his head with his eyes closed. Rubbing his brow between his fingers.

Agni turns to bring out the flower from her bag. She presents it to Rakh, "Not just any flower. This one's rare and has unique uses."

Rakh lets out an exasperated sigh, "You — you have been had by a..."

He stops mid-sentence as he opens his eyes and sees the flower. He quickly covers the flower with the wrapping and puts it back in Agni's bag. He quickly scans the surroundings to make sure no one was observing them.

"Who gave this to you? Did you get his name? Where did he go?" Rakh bombards them with questions one after the other in an excited state. Seeing them shake their heads though, deflates him.

"Very well. You had a narrow escape. This time," he says after calming himself down. "But you have to promise me to be careful about using your powers."

"You cannot trust anyone." He adds ominously. Sunten quickly agrees. Relieved that this interaction did not go too far sideways.

It is completely dark by now. The subtle red haze of Sukarsha covers the night sky.

Rakh starts preparing to take their leave off the caravan. "I have set off three shadow Focus. They should convince anyone observing that we are still inside that wagon. I will raise the suppression field once we put distance between us and the camp. Hopefully the ruse should work."

Neither Sunten, nor the children understand what Rakh has said, but they nod in agreement. Vehemently.

Rakh takes one final look around the caravan camp. He then instructs Sunten and the children to grab their supplies and backpacks and follow him.

Sunten hesitant at first, decides now is not the time to agitate Rakh further. He starts following Rakh away from the caravan. Agni and Dvija in tow. Rakh signals them to stay low and close to him.

As they get farther from the camp, the grass around them keeps getting taller. At one point, it becomes tall enough to hide Sunten, Agni and Dvija. However, Rakh has to crouch a little to stay out of sight. They are carrying enough for a three day journey at least. They will have to forage their way through Null to make the full trip.

> I wish I could share my ample supplies with them. Not like I need everything. Might even make a friend or two in the process.

As Rakh pauses and looks around, Sunten tells the children to wait and moves up to tap Rakh on his shoulder. In return he receives a glare from him, "What now?"

"Erm, R..R...Rakh, are you sure we are doing the right thing leaving the caravan?" Sunten stutters his way through the sentence.

"Look around, there is nothing but grass. One wrong step and the children could get lost here," he says, whispering.

Rakh continues to glare at him. A flicker of regret crosses his face. He is having second thoughts about acquiescing to Sunten's request to accompany them.

"We should stay with the caravan," Sunten says with all the courage he can muster.

Rakh lets out a long drawn sigh, whispering, lest his words upset the children, "All morning you pestered me to avoid the caravan. All afternoon you complained to slow down the caravan. And to top it all, you allowed Dvija to use his power."

Rakh pauses, rubbing his brows, "and now — now you want us to stick with the caravan."

"I promise you Sunten, another word out of you and regardless of what tantrum those two throw, I will leave you behind."

Sunten gulps and takes a step back.

"Now quiet down and let me put up the suppression field. Unless you want your old friends to find us."

Fear passes over Sunten's face.

He moves over to the children. Agni and Dvija huddle up to him.

"Its OK kids, he knows what he is doing. Let's rest for a bit while he works," he says. Comforting the children.

"We will be safe before you know it."

Why does he lie?

Why do all of them lie so blatantly?

Why do they think lying makes it better?

Does it not make the truth even scarier? Difficult to manage?

Is cuddling and cajoling really the only way they know to calm a scared child?

How do you think a child feels when their parent tells them that they will be safe and soon afterwards find themselves hiding beneath corpses of their kin? How does any of these actions make sense?

Chapter 26

I — apologise for my outburst. No matter the reason, I should not have lost control like that. The Chronicle deserves a better Chronicler. You, who are the only one who cares for these records, deserve a better Chronicler. My people need someone worthy to continue their legacy. Not a foolish, scared, child.

Unfortunately, though, all any of you are left with, is me.

So, I continue to labour.

Oh, and do not worry about the occasional stain you see on the pages as you read through. They are nothing but my tears.

They do not smear the written word.

That is all you care about either way.

Chapter 27

Thread: Sunten

Location: Torika wildlands

They are moving again. Rakh a few paces ahead. Sunten and the children maintaining a constant distance between him and them. The caravan's lights quickly fade in the distance. They are moving at a fast pace. They know well the danger they are in.

After the caravan's lights are hidden from sight, Sunten lets out a soft whistle to signal Rakh to stop. Sunten takes out a flask from his side and gives Agni and Dvija a sip each. Rakh approaches them. Unlike earlier, he wears a soft expression. Looking at the children, and then to Sunten.

"I know it is difficult, but we need to keep moving till the first moon reaches zenith."

> It's strange. His words. His voice — it's different — and not. As if two voices speak the words at once. In two different languages.

Must be the suppression field affecting the translation Focus of the Chronicle.

Nothing to be done but hope that Rakh does not talk too much during this mission.

Sunten and the children put on a brave face and start moving.

Rakh springs up and swiftly moves ahead of them. Without stopping, he looks back at them and gives them an encouraging smile.

"Keep moving but stay behind me."

The three give a sheepish grin and step back to maintain a gap between them and Rakh. Since the suppression field has gone up, everything outside it appears to have fallen silent. Even what little I could see through Sunten's one sided vision has also become blurrier.

Sunten is moving with confidence. He is somewhat familiar with these grasslands. Spending time in the badlands as an initiate of the Nirdak. The dangers that lurk here are not new to him. As they move, he is continuously scanning their surroundings. There is a rising feeling of alarm. But he cannot quite put his finger on it. With the limited vision due to the suppression field, he cannot quite place where they are going. And while Rakh is showing his mastery at following the trail, every so often, Sunten keeps having to signal him to change direction to avoid unseen dangers.

After perhaps four turns of the hourglass Rakh signals them to stop. Large shapes loom in the distance. Overhead the first moon is at its zenith.

> Since Sunten and the others left the caravan, they have travelled deep into the grasslands. If I remember Zirsa's map correctly, they are close to the southern Nirdak village near the Null.

Sunten takes out portions of food, and water from his backpack and hands it to Agni and Dvija. He still has a look of concern on his face. The journey to the Torika gap was never supposed to be easy, but something kept nagging at him at the back of his mind. He hunched down to study the trail. Noticing signs of the night predators that pervaded these grasslands. He calls to Rakh, who walks over to them.

"Something is off Rakh," he says, while pointing at the signs he had noted.

"We did not encounter a single predator. For hours. They do not avoid humans. At all."

"You are complaining about having it easy now?" Rakh says dismissively.

"Enough rest. Let's keep moving. I want to be at the gap before daybreak."

Rakh starts moving, before Sunten could press his point. He quickly gathers their bags and nudges the kids to start moving. They are moving in the direction of the large shapes in the distance.

As they get closer, Sunten slows down. Squinting his eye to look at the large blurry shapes. When a sharp whistle pierces the suppression field. Rakh stops instantly. Sunten feels a knot in his stomach. A rising feeling of dread.

The suppression field dissipates for an instant and goes back up. But in that instant, sounds and scents rush in. The large shapes in the distance become clear. And with the clarity comes an overwhelming sense of fear within Sunten.

And me. Read on to find out why.

The large shapes belong to a small village nestled atop a small hillock. With raised walls. A large gate. And everything is charred black.

Sound familiar? It should.

Sunten is looking around frantically. Hands rubbing against his temples. He meets Rakh's silent gaze. His hands reflexively move to Agni and Dvija as he pushes them behind himself. His breathing quickened, he glares at Rakh.

"Why? What...What are we doing here?" Sunten sputters out. Without waiting for a response, he rushes headlong towards Rakh.

"You scum! You are one of them!" he says through clenched teeth. Arms outstretched he goes for Rakh's neck. Rakh deftly sidesteps the rush and brings Sunten down on his back. Rakh pushes down his knee on Sunten's chest and pins down his arm with his hands.

Back where they stand, Agni and Dvija prepare themselves to attack. A small white hot fireball springs up in Agni's hand. Rakh snaps his head up to face them. A smirk forms on his face.

"This is oddly familiar."

Sunten continues to struggle against Rakh to no avail.

"Unless you want all the Nirdak in that village to hurtle down to us, I suggest all three of you calm down."

Dvija at once curls down into a ball on the ground, shaking with fear at the mere mention of the Nirdak. Agni on the other hand, only disperses the fireball in her hand. But she does not take her eyes off Rakh. Her glare strong enough to burn a hole in a lesser person. Shaking with anger at this apparent betrayal.

Sunten starts quietly sobbing into the mud.

"Not again. Why? Take me...Leave them alone."

Rakh bends towards Sunten, his voice dropping to a whisper, but the menace in it at its height, "I said — calm. down."

Sensing the futility of his situation, Sunten quiets down. Going limp in surrender. Rakh raises him up with one hand and pushes him back towards Agni and Dvija. He falls to his knees, unable to speak. His eyes staring helplessly towards Rakh.

> He is reliving his past in his mind. His guilt... His failure... I... I can somehow feel his guilt as if it were my own. Like that last time. It is overwhelming. It is painful. It is impossible for me to be sharing his emotions so strongly. It's not intuition this time. I am actually feeling his emotions. I have been since I Connected to his Thread earlier. I just did not notice till they become overwhelming.
>
> But how? Who is he?
>
> I will have to Delve into his past. The earliest chance I get.

Sunten looks on as Rakh sits in front of them cross legged. Unconcerned at being outnumbered three to one. He has proven himself to be the smarter fighter.

"Why Rakh? Sunten struggles to get the words out his mouth. His breathing laboured. Tears flowing down his eyes.

"I trusted you!"

He turns to look at Agni standing beside him, holding her stance. Dvija, quivering in fear behind him. He looks back at Rakh, voice low, seething with anger.

"They," he says, pointing to the children, "trusted you!"

Rakh meets his gaze. Expressionless.

"I do not like to repeat myself Sunten."

Rakh narrows his eyes, darting them to the left, "But, it's too late to heed my advice now."

A look of confusion crosses Sunten's face as he mirrors Rakh. He can see movement in the grass. Too much for the wind. His confusion is quickly replaced by fear. He pulls Agni and Dvija to himself. Whispering in their ears, "Get ready to run!"

In front of them, as Rakh stands up, he grumbles to himself, "A mantle, for the love of Sukarsha, just once, a mantle."

"Shield them Sunten."

He spreads his hands wide, "we have company."

The suppression field instantly dissipates.

And sounds and scents flood in. All at once. From all directions. They are surrounded.

Nirdak. Tens of them.

Of all the thick headed ideas that he could have made, this one has to be...ugh. I... I... don't even have the words to describe the stupidity. A Chronicler without words! That's how bad this is!

Why bring them here? I am sure he had a good reason, but then why not tell it to them? This is not the kind of surprises people enjoy.

Sunten is in panic. Looking for a spot to run through and escape his worst nightmare. He can see none. He spins around at a sound behind him. A large Nirdak rushes ahead of the rest towards them. A club raised overhead, ready to strike.

As the Nirdak is about to swipe down at Sunten's head, a purple flash appears between them, blinding Sunten for a few moments.

When he can see clearly, he sees the Nirdak laying on the ground, unconscious. Sunten, looks around, and sees purple flashes across the grassland. Each accompanied by a thud or a cry of pain.

A sense of gratitude for Rakh flows through his mind.

Again. I should not be able to feel his emotions so strongly.

Sunten is torn between helping Rakh and keeping the children safe. However, it only takes another instant for him to come to a decision. He looks at the children with a determined look and indicates them to follow him.

While the Nirdak are distracted by Rakh's unpredictable assault, Sunten pulls Agni and Dvija aside and makes a run for it. Away from the village and the Nirdak. Straight towards the Torika Gap.

As the sounds of the battle fade to silence, Sunten slows down. They are scratched across their arms and legs by the fresh blades of grass surrounding them. Panting for breath they come to a stop.

"Sunten," says Dvija, "why did we leave Rakh behind? He was helping us. Didn't you see? He was fighting the Nirdak."

Before Sunten could answer, Agni, jumps in, "hush Dvija, he was helping against them, sure, but he's the one that took us there."

She crosses her arms, a look of regret passes across her face. "We should not have trusted him," she says with finality.

Dvija looks down, unconvinced, but knowing better than to argue with his sister.

Sunten pats Dvija on the head. "Don't worry Dvija. We are here. Together. Is all we need." He brings Agni and Dvija to him in an embrace. "I will always protect both of you."

...I miss them.

A rustling in the grass breaks their moment of peace. Sunten startled, looks around, turning, while keeping the children behind him. He finds the source of the sound.

A man wades through the grass towards them, brandishing a short sword in his hand. A symbol tattooed over his right eye of two hooks crossed like an "X".

The brand of the Nirdak.

His face is unsmiling. Rugged and beaten up. Multiple scars mar his face. His eyes take in all three of them as he slowly approaches them. His lips form a snarl as he speaks in a grating voice, "You must be — Sunten."

Sunten takes a sharp breath. Staring at the face of the Nirdak. Trying to figure out if he recognises him from his past life. But nothing comes to mind. Nothing but confusion.

"How do you know me? Who are you?"

The man lets out a growl, "I know all three of you Sunten," he shifts his glare to the children, "Agni, and Dvija."

Agni who was putting up a brave front till now, recedes behind Sunten when confronted so blatantly by the Nirdak. Pulling Dvija close to herself.

Everything has fallen silent again. The sound of the wind, the scent of the grasslands. Gone.

"You should not be here, but it's too late. Should have stayed silent for your own good," the Nirdak speaks with menace in his voice.

A silent purple flash to the side, Rakh glides in smoothly and crosses between Sunten and the Nirdak, none the worse for his battle. His hands crossed behind his back. Head held high.

"Enough Trinak. I think they have learnt their lesson."

Rakh turns to face Sunten.

"Haven't you?"

A roar of laughter erupts from the Nirdak.

Still confused at the situation, Sunten takes a step back, as if to make a break for it.

Rakh lets out a disappointed sigh, "or I suppose not. Trinak, if you would."

Trinak stops laughing and moves closer to Sunten. He rubs his hands over his face and as he pulls them away, the brand of the Nirdak is not seen. Though the scars remain, he has a gentler look, smiling at Sunten and the children.

He points to his face, “Not a Nirdak.”

Sunten gingerly moves forward and brings his hand up to Trinak’s forehead. A gentle touch and pulls back his hand. Heaving a sigh of relief, he sits on the bare ground with a thump. Agni and Dvija also straighten up. Confused about what is happening, but certain of their safety.

Sunten puts back his head and lets out a loud laughter. Which is instantly cut off by Trinak’s large hand covering his mouth.

“You are right Rakh, he does not learn quickly,” Trinak says to Rakh with an exasperated look.

“Yes, the sooner we are away from the village, the better,” Rakh says, shaking his head.

“Do you have them?” he says to Trinak.

Before responding, Trinak looks at Sunten and wags his finger at him. Then pulls away the hand covering Sunten’s mouth. Satisfied that Sunten is finally in control of himself, he looks to Rakh.

“It took no small effort on my part. And you owe me twice over for reach of these,” he says to Rakh, as he rummages through his pockets.

He finally pulls out an amulet and a bracelet. Both shine as if freshly polished. Intricate symbols engraved across their inner surface. He looks them over for a moment before handing them off Rakh, who looks them over.

Sunten stares at the jewellery and then to Rakh.

Incredulous, Sunten stands up to face Rakh.

"You...you risked our lives for these trinkets?"

He looks to the children, back to Rakh, "This is how you keep your promise to keep them safe?" Sunten raises his hand to punch Rakh. But is quickly blocked by Trinak who twists Sunten's arm behind his back. Sunten struggles and flails around to escape the hold.

Indeed. He does not learn

Rakh raises a hand for Trinak to let Sunten go.

Still staring at Rakh in anger, Sunten pulls himself free of Trinak's relaxed grip with a grunt. Rakh moves to Sunten in an instant, leaning in. Without raising his voice, his face expressionless, Rakh speaks, "Now, I think that little fight with the Nirdak should be proof enough that I will not falter when it comes to keeping the children safe."

Sunten swallows. Intimidated by Rakh's proximity. He gives a reluctant nod.

Rakh continues, "But, If I have to spell out everything. That's not trust. That's you sitting in judgement of my decisions. Trust means putting aside your limited view and believing I'm doing what's best. Correct?"

Sunten gulps before nodding again.

Rakh straightens his back, "These *trinkets* are critical to their survival. Do you want to know why?"

Sunten pauses a moment, before shaking his head.

"Good. A lesson learnt," Rakh says with a smile.

Rakh looks to Trinak, "Thank you for this favour Trinak. This means more than you know."

Trinak blushes and waves off Rakh.

Rakh looks towards the mountain range looming ahead of them. A small vertical slit between them glows with an eerie dim red light.

"We head to the Gap now. Trinak, do inform Zirsa. I dare not lower the suppression field again before entering the Null."

Trinak gives a salute to Rakh by holding a fist across his chest, "Yes, Prime Talon. It will be done."

He turns and runs towards the village. His sounds fade instantly as he passes the threshold of the suppression field.

Sunten, comes up to Rakh, "I apologise for my actions, Rakh. If not earlier, then definitely now you have our complete trust." Beside him Agni and Dvija nod vigorously in acknowledgement.

Rakh looks at the three of them and smiles, “Thank you.”

He looks to the Gap, “But we have delayed enough, and we lost much of our supplies in that ambush. But we must press on.”

Without warning he starts walking towards the Gap. Sunten and the children scramble to follow him.

Chapter 28

Thread: Zirsa

Location: Vaasat

Looks like all the Threads are tearing ahead now. Too fast and too much for me to observe. Even the 10 Step war between Sorni and Korinshan was recorded by three teams of Chroniclers, and the war did not even last an hour.

And look at what we have today, the most important event in the history of the world. The very end of all life in Prathak, and we have half a Chronicler recording it.

If ever you, or anyone else, sit in judgment these Chronicles, know that I did the best I could.

We go back to the Grove of the Talons. There is sure to be a fallout from Rakh's diktat to Zirsa. Their dynamic is something that could potentially fill volumes. You can never tell who commands whom with these two.

Zirsa is standing in her meeting room. Behind her a window looks onto the entirety of Vaasat from a high vantage point. That and the stone based construction of the room suggests she is in the tower in the middle of Vaasat. A simple but large wooden table and an accompanying high chair, occupy one corner of the room. The rest is unadorned by any form of furniture or furnishings, A large door on one end of the room leads to a landing of a spiral staircase going down. There is a smaller door on the other end, but it is closed shut.

In front of her, the faint images of two Talons hover silently. They look at each other before turning to Zirsa. They wait for her to speak.

The one to Zirsa's left has brown skin, while the other is darker still. The brown-skinned Talon is wearing tight, almost form-fitting clothing. Except for a dagger hanging to his side, there is no other adornment on his clothes. He has a lanky build. Standing straight at his full height he is taller than most, perhaps even Rubio, but currently, he stands hunched forward. He has no facial hair to speak of, not even on his head or eyebrows. There is no emotion shown on his face. He has the stance of a soldier. Waiting for his commander to give an order.

Name: Suthrin

Affiliation: Talon

Rank: Agent

The second Talon on the other hand is the complete inverse in just about every manner. He is of a burly build. While clean shaven as well, he does sport a full head of hair, pulled back in a short pony tail at the back. He is decked with multiple types of armaments. Just what is visible to the eye on his loose clothing would be enough to arm a small fighting force. Two swords hang at his waist on each side. Daggers and throwing knives arranged across a belt on his chest. There is a heavy axe on his back as well as a short spear. There are neatly arranged throwing pots hanging across his waist. You can see the hilts of four more daggers jutting out from his high shoes. He is smiling and looking around, uncaring of Zirsa's presence in front of him. He shifts weight from leg to leg every few moments, as if tired of standing for so long, and anxious to move.

Name: Donas

Affiliation: Talon

Rank: Initiate

> How he can stand with all these weapons on his body is beyond me. It is almost as if he would float away if he ever took off all his weapons.

Finally, after a few moments in deep thought, Zirsa looks to them in turn and starts giving instructions.

"I hope you have received the locations that I have sent you."

They both nod in acknowledgement.

"Good. I don't need to tell you how dangerous this can be. He will be completely incommunicado due to the suppression field. Even the Eyes will be unable to find him."

Even though her face is in her usual commanding expression, her voice gives away her internal worry.

Suthrin speaks first. "It shall be as you command Zirsa. We shall leave for the Null immediately. I assure you, we shall be waiting for him," he says in a disciplined tone.

There is a smile on Zirsa's face that does not touch her eyes. "Suthrin," she says with a slight shake of her head, "how many times must I tell you? You are no longer a soldier in the army, and I am most definitely not your commander. I am simply the first among equals. You can speak to me like one."

Donas lets out a snicker. Suthrin shoots a glare at him before turning back to Zirsa. Without any change in his expression or tone, he replies, "As you command Zirsa."

Beside him Donas bursts out into laughter. When both Zirsa and Suthrin look at him in annoyance, he gets flustered and tries to stand straight while suppressing his laughter.

“Donas,” Zirsa says looking straight at him, “I would remind you that while Suthrin is my equal, you most certainly are not his. You are but an initiate yet. He has been a Talon longer than you have been alive. Show him the respect he deserves.”

Donas lowers his eyes, embarrassed. He tries to say something but is only able to sputter out some half words before he covers his mouth with both hands, lest he burst into laughter.

Zirsa gives a slight smile but begins to admonish him again before Suthrin speaks up.

“Zirsa, I would request you to let him be. He has yet to learn a lot. Like how to stay disciplined in a planning session, " he says while casting a sidelong glance at Donas.

Donas shrinks into himself further at the rebuke but stands straight in the next instant. At attention and says, “Apologies Master. I will not embarrass you further.”

Suthrin gives a proud nod and looks to Zirsa. “See, we will make a Talon out of him yet.”

Zirsa looks at Donas and gives a nod.

"As I was saying," she continues, "This will be a dangerous mission. I would have preferred to send more Talons on this mission, but time is of the essence and unfortunately, no one except you two will be able to reach Rakh in time. He will already have to cover a huge tract of Nirdak-controlled territory without any support. But I will not have him travelling through the Null by himself with three extremely strong objects and three civilians in tow."

Suthrin and Donas nod. Before Zirsa can continue, Donas raises his hand with hesitance. Zirsa looks at him with a raised eyebrow. "Donas, you can ask a question if you have one. You do not need to raise your hand before asking one."

Donas gives a sheepish smile and says, "Yes Zirsa. What I wanted to know was why is Rakh using a suppressing field. Nirdak don't have the ability to detect Artefacts or Focus like the Eyes do. And even if they have a Divining focus, they cannot detect unadorned Focus."

On the other side, Suthrin nods his head in agreement. He had thought of this too but was too disciplined to directly question Zirsa like this.

A flicker of shock passes across Zirsa's face. She did not expect this question. Not from Donas at least. Without wasting another moment, she concocts a lie to pacify Donas' curiosity before it spread across the ranks of the Talons.

"The Focus were in Svarka for more than a few days before they were recovered. Not to mention the Artefact had been in Anthala for weeks. The residual power of Anthala could easily activate the Artefact or the Focus. Most likely not fully, but enough for a Divining Focus to detect them. Besides, Rakh's own Focus is bound to him. Even if he does not use it, it will still radiate power."

> See how easy it is for the Talons to lie. Even to their own. Everyone thinks they are some kind of saviour. But we know the truth. You and I.

Donas looks like he wants to ask something more, but Zirsa raises a hand to instruct him. to stop. "We will discuss this further when everyone is safely in the Grove's protection. For now, this is all you need to know. Use what little time you have to prepare. perhaps a short rest. The next few days are going to be very demanding. You will have no time to rest on your journey to Torika, if you are to reach the Null border before Rakh."

Suthrin and Donas nod. While Suthrin does not allow any emotion to touch his face, it is obvious that Donas Is disappointed at the dismissal. He wanted to ask something more.

Zirsa turns the ring on her finger, and the images of the two Talons fade away. All alone in the room, Zirsa lets her emotions come out. She holds herself tight. She is flustered by the whole situation.

It has mostly been a peaceful couple of centuries as far as the Channelers are concerned. Sure, there have been wars between the smaller kingdoms, but for the Channelers it has been the status quo. They were hunted and where possible, the Talons would come to their aid. Nothing out of the ordinary. But this current situation has Zirsa in a bind.

Kintra knocks and enters the room. She stands at the doorway, waiting for Zirsa to begin the conversation.

Zirsa lets out an audible sigh and beckons Kintra to come closer. "You may say what you came here to say Kintra. You do not need my permission every time."

Kintra gives a slight nod. She does not agree with Zirsa, but, neither is she going to argue with her. She simply moves on to the next step.

"Zirsa, the council is arriving in the chambers. The quorum is met. We only need you to begin the meeting. The council—"

Kintra hesitates for a moment before continuing, "The council has gotten word that the Eyes have discovered two new Focus. They anxiously await to discuss the prospective Talons who could be assigned to use these Focus."

Zirsa snaps to look towards Kintra. "I had expected to be able to control the news. But I should have known better. It seems the vines of Vaasat are good for more than decorating our rooms."

Kintra, clearly not understanding the reference, simply nods.

Zirsa shakes her head and gives a rueful smile. "It looks like a hard task has been made harder. The unfortunate truth is that there will be no discussion on prospective Casters. the Focus have already been adorned by two Casters in Svarka. I will give further details during the meeting. But Kintra—"

Zirsa pauses mid-sentence. Unsure how to say what she intends. In a moment of decisiveness, she continues, "Kintra, I will need your aid here. There is a part of the truth I must keep from the Council. And even as my most trusted advisor, I will still have to keep the information from you too."

An expression of shock flashes across Kintra's face. Her usual formal stance has broken down. "But Zirsa..."

Zirsa interrupts Kintra and continues, "I know Kintra. I need not be reminded of my Oath. But it seems that no matter how much a leader struggles to maintain their transparency, a time comes when they have to keep secrets. The crown of leadership has its way of casting an ugly shadow, whether you like it or not."

She sighs in frustration. Unhappy at being forced to go against her oaths.

"I will not order you to support me in my lie by omission. I can simply request your support. You have the ear of your father Sinkar, and he in turn is influential in the Council. If you can convince him, then with me, we will have control of the Council vote on the Focus. I promise as soon as Rakh arrives safely, I will tell you everything."

Kintra winces at Zirsa's last statement. There is an internal conflict going on. Her gaze lowered, she looks side to side. Finally, resuming her stoic expression, she raises her head towards Zirsa. Her eyes looked on accusingly. "Your promises are now meaningless Zirsa."

At the look of concern on Zirsa's face, Kintra continues, "But do not worry. Despite this lapse in your judgement, you continue to have my loyalty. I know that you would never break your word unless it was for the better of us all. That being said, it also tells me that you would break your word, if you felt justified enough."

Zirsa looks away from Kintra. Tears well up in her eyes, but she quickly blinks them away. She turns back towards Kintra and with a nod, walks past her and heads to the meeting room. Behind her Kintra stays rooted in place for a few moments before turning and following Zirsa.

> Zirsa's mention of crowns and the burdens of leadership. Too specific of an example in an era where much of royalty has withered away. It

leads me to believe that she intimately knew or was part of one of the five royal bloodlines still around. Only they can lie and manipulate their followers so easily. Discovering her past will be easier than I thought. And once I do, I will also know the power that hides it from me.

My instinct tells me that this will peel away a layer of mystery that surrounds the attack on my people.

Chapter 29

I am at a difficult crossroad. I have put duty above all in the past few days. Even at the cost of my survival. But now. What lies ahead is a nightmare. I would rather spend an eternity in the void Thread than do what I must.

Allow me to pose you a question. An emotional exercise.

Let's say you could find out something very important — critical — but you would also have to face something you were deathly afraid of. Something you abhor.

And — And. Even if you fight your fears and obtain that information, there was nothing you could do with it. You would have it and know it to be something world-changing, and that is it. Only you would know. No possible way to disseminate it to those who could use it.

What would you do? Would you face your fear and get it? Hope that somehow the Gods would give you the means to use it. Even though you know the Gods to be uncaring brats who could care less about you?

You wouldn't

I knew you wouldn't.

But — you *would* lie to yourself, lie to me. Make yourself to be this noble soul. Fill me with guilt about abandoning my duty, until I capitulated.

Who cares about a child alone in this place?

Who cares that there is already more than enough for him to be for him to be fearful of?

Not you surely. I am only a conduit of information for you. Nothing more.

So, let's get on with this.

This Thread has been pulsing bright long before I began writing about Rakh's escapades in Anthala. But of late it has taken a new hue, the likes of which I have not seen before. Its bright red. Possibly from being ignored for so long. Or maybe something unworldly. Like the void Thread.

A Thread that belongs to a Nirdak.

And not just any Nirdak.

He is evil incarnate.

Their leader Yapran.

I shudder to Connect to this Thread. But to sate your thirst for knowledge and your blatant overtures about fulfilling one's sacred duty, I must.

You pitiless wretch.

Chapter 30

Thread: Yapran

Location: Ruins of Agni and Dvija's village

Yapran is standing in a makeshift arena. Around him an audience of more than a hundred Nirdak stand in stunned silence. Beyond them are the charred ruins of a village. It is in complete ruin. The houses, the vegetation, the blockade. Everything is burnt to a crisp. And in these ruins, the Nirdak have established a makeshift base. Tents and shelters created in a haphazard manner.

> Seeing it through the Connection is just as haunting as experiencing it through the void Thread. Maybe more so.

Coming back to Yapran, he is facing down three opponents. Three other Nirdak. They have him surrounded in the middle. All three, are built like an ox. Broad shoulders. Rippling muscles. They are bare-chested. Wearing only tight trousers. Caked with dirt from the arena floor. They bleed from various wounds and injuries on their faces and bodies. Their loud panting the only sounds heard. Weary and injured, they are glaring at Yapran in the middle. Warily circling, but ready to pounce at a moment's notice.

Yapran himself is not too different from his three opponents. Similar broad shoulders and rippling muscles. He is completely bald. Face covered in a thick beard. His eyes have a cruel glint in them. There is no sign of fatigue in his movements. Even with three strongmen bearing down on him, he is not showing a hint of fear. He looks from one to another baring his teeth at them in a wide grin.

Before the three can completely close in on him, he speaks to them with derision, "So, you three still think you can take me on?"

The confidence and spite in his voice give the three strongmen reason to pause their advance. They stop and glance at each other. Without warning, the one facing Yapran head on leaps towards him. Not wasting another moment, the other two lunge forward as well.

Yapran smiles and crouches to brace himself against the floor. As the first strongman nears, Yapran snaps forward and grabs the man. Effortlessly lifting the man off his feet and using the man's momentum to swing on the balls of his feet, he throws him directly into the two men attacking from the other side. All three crash into the arena floor.

None of them have the strength to get back up.

"You three believed that one of you could replace me? The mighty Yapran?"

As he speaks, he walks over to them.

Laying on the arena floor in a broken pile.

"Do. Not. Forget. Who. You. Are. Dealing. With."

With every word, he kicks one of the three men in the ribs. Their cries of pain piercing the silence.

"I am your Master," he yells and brings down his foot with force on one of the three's legs. An audible snap is heard. Yapran steps away and spits on the ground in front of him. He turns towards the audience and lets out a roaring laughter. The crowd, silent so far, starts cheering him on with great vigour.

> Sadists all of them. I hope you are satisfied. Forcing me to watch these scum inflict such violence. If you thought I was jesting about being terrified about Connecting to this Thread, I hope this little show sways your opinion!
>
> Oh! Who am I trying to convince? You do not care. No one does.

Yapran abruptly stops laughing and points towards the three broken men. "This is the fate of all those who deem to rise against me."

The crowd goes silent once more. No one dares move or say anything. Yapran points towards two amongst the audience and beckons them. He points towards the three fallen Nirdak and makes a slashing gesture at his wrist. The two men from the audience, gulp and share a glance at each other. They rush forward without a word and go about trying to take the three injured men away from the arena.

A member of the crowd hands Yapran his shirt. He puts it on and walks out of the arena. The crowd parts away to let him through. The ones right along the edge bow down as he passes by. He walks to a raised platform with a large high-back chair on it. There are lit torches surrounding the platform. The flickering light gives an ominous look to the chair which is adorned with several crude objects. Layer upon layer, they adorn the chair's back and part of its armrests unevenly. Perhaps done by an amateur. Other than these bizarre shapes, the chair seems to be made of simple wood.

As Yapran takes his seat, the crowd somehow regain their voice too. They start cheering. Yapran postures for the crowd. Looking around at the faces of those gathered. He raises his hand in the air with a triumphant fist. The crowd is further riled up. Yapran opens his fist to ask for silence. Within moments the crowd falls silent. Not a sound can be heard, except for a blood-curdling distant yell.

Men such as Yapran, thrive on the knowledge that they control others. The more control the better. This little gesture of silencing the crowd probably gave him goosebumps of happiness. I only hope this control sates his violent tendencies. I do not want to see anything worse than I have already....

Oh no! Oh no no no! No! Curse you!

The shapes on the throne. I know what they are now.

The two men who had left with Yapran's incapacitated opponents earlier have returned. They are carrying something in their hands. They walk up to Yapran's throne. They stand with bowed heads, waiting for his signal. He looks at them and nods his head. They step up to the throne. They look for clear unadorned space on the throne. Finding it on the armrest, they start hammering an object to its outer edge.

I do not want to describe this any further. I cannot. Seeing this is offensive enough. But to sully the Chronicle with this desecration.

I must though. Mustn't I?

Yes.

Its hands.

The objects the two men carry are hands, three pairs, carelessly dissected at the wrists. From the three men who lost their fight against Yapran.

The hands — they are being nailed to the chair. And covered with some kind of resin.

This is Yapran's choice of adornment — hands of poor souls who dared to stand against Yapran. There are too many to count.

Yapran looks on. The glint in his eyes, the cruelty on his face. unbecoming of any living creature.

As the last of the hands is caked in resin, the two men step away and join the crowd. Everyone waits with bated breath for Yapran's words. He stands and walks to the edge of the platform.

"You are not worthy of calling yourselves Nirdak."

Contempt in his voice. His face turned up in disgust.

"Not one of you could prevent the traitor Sunten from escaping. That too with the two survivors. Inconsequential survivors, no doubt, yet a humiliating loss. Even the Talons fear facing us alone and a cripple escaped from under your noses."

He pauses for a moment, a slow anger rising in him, "I should have destroyed this pathetic camp as soon as I got here. Only the strategic advantage of us being near the Null and Svarka has stayed my hand so far. But you — you should have begged me to put you out of your misery. For being an insult to our name."

Yapran strikes a young man standing in front of the platform. The man stumbles back into the crowd bringing others down with him. No one makes to help any of those who fell, lest they portray sympathy for the weak.

Yapran continues with a sneer, "You are weak. All of you. Pathetic bugs, to be squashed under the boot of your betters. Yet — your captains thought to take on me. Take on the leadership of the Nirdak!"

He lets out a derisive laughter. He turns to point at his throne. Without turning to the crowd, he speaks, a hint of reverence in his voice, "This throne belongs to the leaders of the Nirdak. Each leader adorns it with the hands of their enemies. Today your captains' hands join those of our enemies. A first in our history. A shameful event. Yet it is so."

He turns back to the crowd, glaring at them, "But, you cheered me on while they fell. You have no loyalty to incompetence and for that, I give you another chance. I have information that two new Focus have surfaced in Svarka. No doubt the Talons would have Seen them before us. It is a race against time. These Focus must be brought under our control. Fail me again and not one of you will live to see another rising of the sun."

He gives a dismissive gesture and turns away from the crowd. The crowd starts to shuffle away, when a low growling voice carries across them, "Find me the Focus or die!" They all heard it as if the voice whispered into their very ears. In moments a sudden energy ripples through the crowd, and they rush out of the arena to deal with their life-or-death task.

Leaving Yapran sitting alone in his precious throne. Contemplating his next action, when a shimmering figure forms right in front of him. He gives no sign of surprise. As if the appearance of the figure was expected.

Yapran gives a deferential bow towards the figure, "Lord Ucharas."

There is a subtle glow around the figure. Just a hint of incorporeality. Fully formed it appears to be a tall man. He is dressed in tattered robes, but it is clear that they were once immaculate and regal. Subtle gold threads woven through the cuffs and lapel. There is a large emblem embroidered on the right side.

It seems familiar, but I cannot recall how.

It is the only part of the cloth that looks complete and unaffected by wear and tear like the rest of his clothes. Unkempt silver hair falling to his shoulders. His skin is wrinkled. Wrinkles upon wrinkles. However, despite his apparent age, he stands straight. No sign of weakness. He holds himself with dignity, head held high. Not even acknowledging Yapran's bow.

> Don't ask me who he is. He is Lord Ucharas I presume. Is it a title? a name? I do not know. I cannot Glean him. Once again, another entity shielded by an unknown power. I shall simply stop using Gleans going forward. Save my energy for more important things.

He turns away and casts a gaze around the empty outpost.

"I see you have had your usual effect here Yapran," he sneers.

Yapran lets out a grunt at the snide remark. He gets up from his chair and stands next to Ucharas' image, head bowed down, but a hint of defiance in the way he stands.

Ucharas looks away. His head raises upwards. Looking at the subtle disturbances that play on Sukarsha's surface. A sign of the magical storms hammering away at it.

> The disturbances look larger today. More frequent too.

"It will all be over soon, Yapran," Ucharas says with a hint of longing in his voice.

"No more Sukarsha, no more Talons and no more interference from that pesky Rakh."

That tone. It sounds personal.

And yes, I am more surprised about him having a personal vendetta with Rakh than the fact that he thinks Sukarsha will be gone soon. Did I not mention that the core tenet of the Nirdak is that Sukarsha is a prison rather than a shield?

That they believe they are the chosen saviours.

That they will liberate us from this prison.

Ignore the fact that thousands of years of recorded Chronicles state otherwise. That the devastation would be total. Insanity comes in various forms. Am I any less insane than them?

The only difference — theirs is going to be fatal.

Yapran looks to Ucharas. A hint of surprise on his face.

"Rakh, lord? Why do you concern yourself with him?"

Ucharas does not move his gaze from Sukarsha.

"Concern yourself to the task at hand. Nothing more. I was expecting two Focus to be handed over to me. I recall a great deal of posturing and chest-thumping. Yet here I stand. Two Focus short."

He looks directly at Yapran. Contempt in his eyes.

"Do not fail me Yapran. I had given ample warning. Yet the Focus slipped through your hands. And — you let that traitor Sunten escape the oath."

Yapran stiffens for a moment at Sunten's mention.

"Yes, I know of him. Do not think it a simple matter to hide things from me. I see all"

Ucharas' eyes bore a hole into Yapran. Even with his head bowed, he can feel the contemptuous gaze upon him.

> Serves him well. So, there's someone out there that even the great Yapran fears.

"You are worthless," Ucharas says while towering over Yapran. The air around him is crackling with lightning. He raises his head as he says this, there is lightning moving along his veins. They collect at his eyes. It looks as if a storm is forming inside his eyes. He floats off the ground, lightning pouring down from his feet towards the ground. Pooling around him like water.

"Despair at your helplessness, boy," he says with a cackling laughter.

> He is looking straight at me. He cannot see me. I am not there. I am safe.

> But...the lightning, the royal clothes. The emblem. I recognise it now. It is impossible. It cannot be him. He is dead, they are all dead and long gone. They died to give life to Sukarsha. But it is him. He is...

"Ucharas, the Lightning Emperor"

Hands spread, lightning crackling out of his fingertips, out of every pore of his being.

"My confinement has ended. And you shall serve me till the end of your days."

Yapran stands there, befuddled at the strange actions of his master.

> He does not know the truth of his Master. That is why I cannot Glean him. But I do. I know him now and there is nothing I can do with it. No one I can share this information with.
>
> Curse Ucharas!
>
> Curse the gods!
>
> Curse the Krihaani!
>
> Curse you!
>
> You — you forced me here. I warned you. I shared my fear of the knowledge I would gain here, yet you forced me here. A lonesome boy who lost his family, and friends. Everyone he knew. And you still forced him to face this.
>
> Enough! The Chronicle ends here. I will write no more to sate your ugly desire for knowledge.

8th Day of Sinter, Year 10277 3rd CE

Here ends Volume XC-3211

Epilogue

7th Day of Sinter, Year 10277 3rd CE

The young Chronicler flounders at his duty.

He allows emotion to creep into the Chronicle.

He violates its purpose.

The Chronicle is not a tale. It is a record of events. Plain and simple.

He has disconnected from a Thread because he loses interest in it.

Unacceptable.

Here I lay the record for the Connection as it should be in the vision of the first Grand Chronicler.

Thread: Rakh

Location: Svarka

Event Designation: Knot (Minor)

Other Threads present: Rubio, Sunten, Agni, Dvija

Sunten has summarised the events where he participated in an attack on Agni and Dvija's village. He believes it to be a coincidence. Rakh further questions him about the use of Agni and Dvija's conversion into living Focus. An occurrence thought to be impossible by all present.

Rakh reaches the conclusion that he, Sunten, Agni and Dvija should leave Svarka post haste and make their way to Vaasat. He acknowledges the difficult of travelling with children and considers spending the night to make necessary preparations.

Rubio has concerns about his brother, Ardeo who is also a high placed leader in the Nirdak cult. Rakh reassures him and leaves Rubio and Sunten to continue their conversation.

Before making the preparations, Rakh exits the bounds of Svarka to report to his superior: Zirsa of the Talons. After speaking to Zirsa he contacts an unknown Talon and gives him instructions to retrieve two objects from a nearby village.

Thread disconnected.

Delves Needed: None

Threads for further examination: Rubio, Ardeo

Keywords: Vaasat, Talon, Svarka, Clandestine

9th Day of Sinter, Year 10277 3rd CE

The young Chronicler allows his emotions to override his purpose.

He refuses to continue the duty given to the Krihaani.

Time since last Connection: 24 hours.

Last Chronicler Protocol initiated.

About the Author

Kanwal Kapoor studied at Georgia Tech and worked with global companies before founding his own animation studio, collab orating with Disney and Discovery Kids. A lifelong reader, he has spent years shaping the expansive universe of Prathak, now debuting with his first fantasy novella. Kanwal enjoys books, games, and long walks that keep his imagination alive.

You can connect with me on:

https://www.kanwalkapoor.ink

https://www.instagram.com/kanwalkapoor7

The Story Continues with...

Coming Summer 2026!

Printed at Repro India Ltd.